T0328744

The
REUNION

The
REUNION

Novelization by
DANIEL JOSEPHS

Story by
MIKE PAVONE

Screenplay by
MIKE PAVONE

World
Wrestling
Entertainment®
BOOKS

POCKET BOOKS

New York   London   Toronto   Sydney   New Delhi

Pocket Books
A Division of Simon & Schuster, Inc.
1230 Avenue of the Americas
New York, NY 10020

This book is a work of fiction. Names, characters, places, and incidents either are products of the author's imagination or are used fictitiously. Any resemblance to actual events or locales or persons, living or dead, is entirely coincidental.

Copyright © 2011 by World Wrestling Entertainment, Inc.

World Wrestling Entertainment, the names of all World Wrestling Entertainment televised and live programming, talent names, images, likenesses, slogans and wrestling moves, and all World Wrestling Entertainment logos and trademarks are the exclusive property of World Wrestling Entertainment, Inc. Nothing in this book may be reproduced in any manner without the express written consent of World Wrestling Entertainment, Inc.

This book is a publication of Pocket Books, a division of Simon & Schuster, Inc., under exclusive license from World Wrestling Entertainment, Inc.

All insert photos copyright © 2011 World Wrestling Entertainment, Inc. All rights reserved.

First Pocket Books paperback edition October 2011

POCKET and colophon are registered trademarks of Simon & Schuster, Inc.

For information about special discounts for bulk purchases, please contact Simon & Schuster Special Sales at 1-866-506-1949 or business@simonandschuster.com.

The Simon & Schuster Speakers Bureau can bring authors to your live event. For more information or to book an event, contact the Simon & Schuster Speakers Bureau at 1-866-248-3049 or visit our website at www.simonspeakers.com.

Designed by Kyle Kabel

Manufactured in the United States of America

10 9 8 7 6 5 4 3 2 1

ISBN 978-1-4767-1103-4

The
REUNION

the
REUNION

Chapter
ONE

Los Angeles, California: City of Angels, city of nothing. Ten million people living fast and breathing smog with no connections, no problems, no ties. A bustling city spread out from coastland to farmland to desert townships, from water to drought. The only chain that linked the desperate and disparate neighborhoods of this wide, sprawling town was the long, heavy arm of the Los Angeles Police Department, an unlikely, violent unifier for a dysfunctional city. Los Angeles was informally known as the "Gang Capital of the Nation," and so it was no surprise that the authorities acted accordingly, earning a reputation for being one of the most violent forces in the country. Even now, almost twenty years after the race riots prompted by the Rodney King trial, the city was still on edge, walking the thin line between racial sensitivity and an authoritative stance over such a wide swatch of neighborhoods, races, and cultures. All the PR in the world couldn't change the past, but it could inform what came next. It could help the large force adapt and prepare for the changing landscape of the future, regardless of the violent undertones of the city.

Detective Sam Carey knew that, and perhaps that's what drew him into the line of work. On the force it was often hit first, ask questions later—not that different from what he saw growing up. But that was years ago.

The downtown skyline was all glass and steel, all the better to reflect the constant California sunlight. Brutal traffic perpetuated the smog that seemed to reach all the way to the ocean, the noises from the cars and trucks the only organic symphony Los Angeles could truly call its own.

Most of that was evident to Sam, who sat uncomfortably in the small, wobbly chair, his muscled frame towering over the cheap steel and fabric. His boss, Captain Haymer, sat across from him, his face set in the usual scowl. His words droned on but Sam wasn't listening; his eyes traveled to the open window, the dirty square framing the view of glaring sunlight and glass buildings beyond. He knew he should be paying closer attention to the angry noises coming from his captain, but something was distracting him like a rock in his shoe: an errant thought of his younger brother, Leo, even though they hadn't spoken in well over ten years. Theirs had not been an easy childhood, which probably explained the ten-year gap in communication. But one memory stuck in Sam's mind: the little boy with the loud voice and terrified eyes looking up at Sam, his older brother. Hit me, he remembered, the words repeated over and over again. *Hit me, hit me, hit me . . .*

Captain Haymer's booming voice brought him back to the present, to the small, stuffy room, where the captain had set up a flat-screen television monitor on which to view Sam's latest indiscretion. A couple of the other wonks from the force, officers who should have been out preserving the peace or at least grabbing a sandwich at their favorite spot two blocks away, stood in the corner of the room, only thinly veiling their smiles now that Sam once again had been called to the carpet.

"My God, man, but you did hit that sumbitch sweet . . ." Captain Haymer's words trailed off, his eyes remaining glued to the screen.

Sam registered his boss's face, sensing a bit of pride in his words, before looking again at the flat-screen television sitting on the table beside them. Frozen on the screen was the frenzied face of a madman, a towering block of muscle and flesh with wild, crazy eyes. Sam hadn't seen that look in a long time: the hard, open stare, a violence he could feel through the still image. Worse, he barely recognized his own face.

Captain Haymer unfroze the image and re-wound the scene—a bright day, the steps outside the Los Angeles courthouse, the grass surrounding it a vivid green. He watched some lowlife in a cheap suit gloating about a victory before a twin set of news cameras that were all too eager to record the scene that was about to happen. From behind, Sam, blatantly ignoring the news cameras and the fact that they would be recording him, charged at the unidentified man, sweeping him up in the wake of his fury and placing his massive right shoulder squarely in the man's chest. The man was airborne for almost two seconds before Sam sent him crashing to the ground: the perfect tackle. On any given Sunday, on any football field in the country, he would be labeled a hero. But not today. And not in Los Angeles.

Captain Haymer ran the scene back a few more times, watching the violent act over and over again as Sam became increasingly uneasy in his chair. The two other cops in the room continued to laugh and collar each other, completely amused by the scene repeating on the screen. Haymer played and replayed the point of impact until Sam once again could feel the physical force on his chest, the contact of taking the scumbag down. He tried to slow his breathing and remain calm.

Captain Haymer paused the scene and let out a long sigh, his dark hands falling slowly to his desk. His eyes looked weary.

"Did you have to jack him up on national TV?" Captain Haymer asked.

Sam almost didn't know what to say. They'd been here before and it wasn't a new story, not for him. Angry cop. Guilty perp. The system letting the guilty go free. It happened every day in Los Angeles. Sam was sick of it.

Nonetheless, Sam measured his words carefully. "I was . . ." he said, pausing to let his eyes scan the room, "frustrated."

Wrong word. The captain pointed his remote at the monitor, which still held Sam's wild and crazy face, as if it would be frozen that way forever.

"Frustrated? You look like the poster boy for bipolar disorder." The captain's voice was flat and measured, as if he, too, knew they'd been here before.

Sam noticed his boss's calm and made the decision to go on the offensive. "This guy rapes a ten-year-old and gets off?" He paused to steady his voice. "I got a ten-year-old."

Captain Haymer grew quiet then and stared at his desk. Sam looked at him pleadingly, but they did not make eye contact.

"Well, I just wish you woulda killed him," Captain Haymer finally said. "It would have taken the sting out of losing my best cop. I'll need your gun, et cetera."

Sam pulled his ID from his jeans pocket and threw it on the desk, letting it bounce across the polished wood. He let the gun go more slowly, pulling it gently from his belt holster.

Captain Haymer grabbed them both, clearly eager to get this task over with. For the first time,

Sam felt worried. He'd been in trouble before—too much aggression, too quick to get physical with a suspect out in the field—but never like this. Never suspension.

"I will try to clean this up and get you back on the job ASAP." The captain didn't sound very hopeful.

But Sam ignored him, thinking already of what a suspension would mean for his career. For his paycheck. He was a good cop, he knew it. It wasn't his fault the system let scumbags walk free around the city. Sam knew what justice meant, and he knew how to make those who were guilty pay the price for their deeds.

Just then a uniformed officer stuck his head in the doorway to Captain Haymer's office. The captain looked up expectantly, but the officer gestured with his head toward Sam.

"Sorry, Cap. Sam, your sister called. She wanted you to call right back."

A strong uneasiness began to grow in Sam's stomach. First the out-of-the-blue thought of Leo and now a phone call from Nina? Sam suddenly had the sense that if Nina was looking for him, getting suspended was not going to be the worst part of his day.

Chapter
TWO

Not far from the skyscrapers and bustle of downtown, in one of the many quiet, run-down neighborhoods that wend their way throughout the county, Nina Carey sat in her car staring down at her lap. She fingered the silver cross on a chain around her neck, an old habit since childhood, hoping to still the slight shaking in her hands. It usually calmed her down, but not today. She whispered a prayer and reached for the car door handle.

She crossed the busy street, rusted boxes of metal and worn-down wheels speeding by on their way to join the snakes of traffic all around the city. Raising a hand to block out the glaring sunlight, she wished she hadn't forgotten her sunglasses. She walked by the bare patches of grass and dirt, up the cracked sidewalk in front of the complex of shabby condos. Each looked the same, each, somehow, in similar disrepair: faded paint, unkempt lawns, torn screen doors covering entryways that were used to being kept shut and locked.

She walked the familiar path to the painted brown door with the gold X still hanging in its center. She wiped a bit of dust from the dull gold, another habit. From her small purse she pulled out her keys and inserted one into the lock. She had to wiggle the knob and pull up on the door before it opened.

Nina walked into the front room of the condo, forcing out a deep sigh that forecast a chance of tears. On the small table near the front door sat an envelope, sealed and unmailed, addressed in a shaky script. One lone lamp with a yellow shade stood near the closet.

Nina shut the door and adjusted the purse strap on her shoulder, once again fingering the silver cross around her neck. She looked around the room as if seeing it for the first time: the pale yellow walls, a shade she once favored; the brown corduroy couch where her father liked to take naps; the red-and-brown plaid pillows she found for him at a yard sale in the Valley last summer; the old oil painting of an eighteenth-century street in London, a scene the old man curiously loved. Even with all these things, these familiar items, her father's condo now seemed empty. Nina felt tears form in her eyes, but she fought them back, taking another deep breath.

She walked slowly around the front room of the condo, trying to remember the last time she saw her father, the last words he spoke to her, some little bit of their time together that she might be able to carry with her. But nothing came. She was too troubled by her own thoughts, her own plans, since hearing the news of his death. She was a good Catholic girl. She would confess her sins in the end if, indeed, the end failed to justify the means.

She moved over to the dusty table near the couch and noticed the photograph: taken recently, a close-up of her father. He was smiling for the camera, but his eyes looked tired, the glare of the sunlight off his thick glasses too severe. She ran a finger across the glass as if to comfort him. It was the only photograph she could find in the entire condo—nothing of her or Sam or their brother, Leo. Only him, alone as always, forever preserved in dust and glass.

Tears once again built in her eyes, but this time she let them come. "Despite everything, I love you, Daddy," she said. Her voice wavered and caught in her throat. "But this is not going to be easy."

She placed the photo back on the table a bit too harshly. The sound of it hitting the wood echoed across the quiet space. She wiped her eyes and turned away from the photo.

She just hoped that, in the end, it would be worth it.

Chapter
THREE

The black limousine snaked through the streets of downtown, its chrome rims shining in the morning sun. It made a long, languid left turn past Figueroa Street and soon joined the rows of short cars in the traffic of the morning commute. The smell of gas mixed with the smog already choking the morning air. Car horns blared at one another.

None of the noise was apparent inside the quiet confines of the limousine. The tinted windows kept the sun at bay, and the air-conditioning, noiseless and powerful, kept the black leather interior cool and soft. Kyle Wills, having become used to such luxury, read over the *Wall Street Journal* business section and hardly gave it a second thought. What also hardly received a second thought was his young son, Janson.

The boy was a spitting image of his father: fair hair, slender waist, pale blue, inquisitive eyes. Both were dressed for success—Kyle in his dark gray Armani suit, Janson in the dark sports coat and khakis preferred by the Catholic school he attended, one of the best in the city. Janson wasn't sure if his family was Catholic, but according to the other kids in his class, it was money—not faith—that drove the private school. Dollars, not God, dictated their world.

Janson picked at a thread on his coat sleeve, sneaking glances at his father. Kyle Wills cut an intimidating figure. In his midforties, he was slender and strong, with few wrinkles marring his wide forehead and a full head of silver-and-blond blooming hair. Janson's father pored over the newspaper, never looking up, never noticing the boy was in the elegant car with him.

Janson cleared his throat, trying to get his father's attention. He knew not to bother his father when he was reading, especially during their morning drive, but this couldn't wait any longer.

Finally, Janson spoke. "It's due tomorrow."

Wills turned a page of the paper, his eyes staying focused on the small black print, calculating in his head how much profit the numbers of the day foretold. He waited a beat, as if he had only just heard his son's voice.

"What's due tomorrow?" Wills asked, barely audible.

Janson shifted in his seat, glad to have even a scrap of his father's attention and intending to hold on to it as long as he could. Even though he was only in middle school, the boy had learned that if he found an opening, he'd better take it.

"My paper—'What My Dad Does for a Living.' It's due tomorrow." Janson forced the words out as quickly as he could and waited expectantly for a response.

A bodyguard glanced from father to son and shifted uncomfortably in the seat across from them. The hulking figure—one of two in the limousine, dressed identically in dark suit and tie—turned his attention out the window, pretending to scan the street for unseen dangers.

In the front, the driver and the other bodyguard went about their business as well. They all knew their job was to provide security and comfort but to stay invisible to the man they were hired to protect. And not to get involved in personal family business.

Janson continued to stare at his father, waiting for some reply to his comment. He had spent three nights staring at a blank screen on his new MacBook Pro. For all the nice things in their life—the private school, the mansion complete with a new swimming pool, the hired car and driver, the bodyguards, the new laptop—Janson had no idea where they came from. His friends had already finished their papers, long, detailed accounts of lawyers, doctors, state judges, and even a bestselling author. But Janson had nothing. No clues, no stories.

Wills didn't lift his eyes from the paper.

"Oh, yeah," he began. "I, ah, I own a company that . . . owns a lot of other companies."

Another opening. Janson took it. "What kind of companies?" he asked.

"Well," Wills continued, his eyes still glued to the paper, "retail mostly. Clothes, shoes, pharmaceuticals, some high-tech stuff . . ." Wills's voice faded as he became engrossed in an article about the long-term financial effects of the Japanese tsunami on the global marketplace.

"Okay," Janson said, becoming confused. "But what do you actually *do*?"

Wills smiled at the boy's emphasis on the word *do*. "I make money," he said definitively. "It's difficult to explain to someone your age."

Janson stared at his father, feeling both angry and dismissed at the older man's words. It was yet another conversation between them without eye contact. He wondered if this was how his friends had completed their papers. If they had to sit quietly and wait for their chance to pry enough details from their fathers to write a dumb essay complete with thesis statement and follow-up evidence. If they had to sit surrounded by bodyguards just to get a ride to school in an embarrassing monstrosity, when everyone else in town was going green and driving a Prius.

Janson waited for his father to say more, but Wills was already engrossed in another article. Janson had lost his chance. His window of opportunity had closed.

The boy gave up and looked out the tinted window of the sleek car at the traffic all around them. *Where are all these people going?* he wondered. *Somewhere,* he noted. *Anywhere but here.*

Chapter
FOUR

The sounds of traffic were a distant echo across most of downtown, past the flower district with its merchandise already wilting in the strong morning sun; past the jewelers and market stalls hawking imitation goods with fake designer labels; past the Mexican shops offering white lace *quinceañera* dresses and head scarves; past the taco trucks and their tinned mariachi music. There, in the eastern tip of downtown, barely in the shadow of the mighty glass-and-metal towers, sat a street of quiet decrepitude. Buildings filled with bachelor apartments—little more than a room and a dirty lightbulb hanging from the middle of the ceiling—dotted the street. A few storefronts were boarded up and abandoned. Most of the dealers had even made for better digs, able to get a few dollars more for their street bags over on the west side, closer to the ocean, closer to the money.

Amid the disrepair sat a dirty brick-front building. It was small and smelled of mold and cigars, infused in the constant red neon glow of its signage: *Bail Bonds Open 24 Hours.* But most important, for Leo Carey, it was home.

The empty alley echoed Leo's angry shouts, a familiar sound for the few neighbors the bail bondsman had left. Leo was in a dirty business, and everyone down the block and up the next knew he liked to yell.

"You're going back to a guy whose idea of romance is two-for-one night at the dog track?" Leo yelled into the phone, a slow simmer of anger rising underneath the surprise in his voice. He kicked the wood paneling on the wall and watched it shake. It, like everything else in the office, looked worse for the wear. Light switches that only occasionally worked. File cabinets that squeaked bloody murder when they opened, if they opened at all. Two cloudy windows with a view of only the alley and the bums who liked to sleep there in the afternoon.

Leo turned his attention back to the call, fumbling to say the right thing. "Okay, listen. I'm right here, okay? And I treat you like a goddess." He waited a beat to process the words coming into his ears. "What do you mean 'maybe that's my problem'? Hey, I can be a bad boy, too, if that gets you off."

He heard the beep on the line that told him he had another incoming call. Leo pushed all his anger into his stomach in a last-ditch effort to sound tough. His neighbors were going to love this one.

He let his voice go as loud as he could. "Hold on, I'm getting another call!" His scream echoed off the cheap wood paneling. God, he sounded crazy. He sounded like his brother, Sam.

His new persona did not have the anticipated effect. And so Leo was once again in the familiar position of backpedaling. "No, no, no, sweetheart. I'm being a bad boy. Okay? It's like a role-play thing. Ah, hold on. I'm sorry, hold on."

The insistent beep once again came into his ear. Leo clicked the button to get the other call.

"Make it quick, okay?"

Leo Carey had received a lot of bad news in his life. He was a bail bondsman, for Christ's sake.

He heard the worst of the worst: sob stories, deportation tales, long, complicated explanations of how his various clients and scumbags were innocent of all the trumped-up charges brought against them by a system too corrupt and complicated to care about the truth. But never had Leo heard this: the worst news ever. The bottom fell out of his world. He was going to be ruined.

Leo's expression quickly turned to one of rage.

"What do you mean Rodriguez is gone? Do you mean *gone* gone? Because if that's the kind of gone you're talking about, I would appreciate it if you drove down here and shot me in the face, because it would be very comforting for me to be dead right now!"

Leo tried to wrap his head around what this meant. Rodriguez gone. Bail bond lost. All of Leo's money: gone.

Just then Leo heard the tiny squeak of his office door. Mikey, his ancient postman, hobbled into the room. He watched Leo's tirade continue without missing a beat. He, too, knew Leo liked to yell.

"Hey, Leo," the mailman said.

"Hey, Mikey," Leo replied.

"Leo, special delivery," the old man said,

handing over a specially marked, thin, white envelope along with the other mail.

The postman shuffled out of the room as Leo returned to his screaming into the phone. As he listened to the caller's reply, he absentmindedly sifted through the stack of mail, noticing the one with the special-delivery notification. He began to tear open the envelope.

"Rodriguez is the biggest bail I've laid out in my entire life-sucking, miserable career and . . ." Before he could complete the thought, Leo's eyes shifted down to the paper he was holding in his hand. He stopped cold. His mind raced. He reread the words, allowing his brain to soak in their meaning.

"Hold on a second . . ." he said into the phone. He ignored the voice yelling at him from the other end of the line. The entire world transformed itself into this one sheet of paper. This one bit of good fortune. *Special delivery indeed,* Leo thought.

Leo turned back to the phone, a giant smile spreading across his face.

"You know what . . . it's only money."

With that, Leo hung up the phone. He gripped the letter gently, as if holding a precious artifact.

For the first time in a long while, Leo felt that things were finally turning around. He wanted to scream out the news, to yell as loudly as he could so every person on the block would know. But Leo restrained himself. This was one little secret he decided to keep to himself.

Chapter
FIVE

Roughly twenty miles northeast of the state capital of Sacramento sat the legendary Folsom State Prison. It was the second oldest prison in the state, dating back to 1880, but perhaps made famous by Johnny Cash, whose two concerts there in the late 1960s brought Folsom to the forefront of pop-culture trivia. Douglas Carey grew up listening to those Cash records—the singer's deep, gravelly voice set against the tinny recording equipment—and Folsom Prison took on, in the young boy's mind, an almost iconic status. That is, until he had to live there.

What Douglas hadn't realized was how much desert and flatland existed in California, how a state known for fake tits and beaches was actually filled up in the middle with flat, barren plains and shit-filled farms that broadcast their smells depending on which way the wind blew. It was another misconception of his, one following the other—Folsom and now California—and Douglas felt he was behind bars because of those two mistakes, rather than the petty theft charges that brought him here.

He was only twenty years old, a product of Child Services and the state-run system, a juvenile delinquent who once learned the name of his father but never met the man himself. No matter—nothing much ever bothered Douglas Carey, and that ease displayed itself all over his body. Trim with an athletic physique, Douglas used his long, blond hair and cool, blue eyes to pull himself through life, to get the most favors he could from a world that seemed not to give much thought to him at all. No family, no problem. Douglas made do. And he had a good time in the process.

He lay back on the bed, his arms resting behind his head, listening to the sounds of the minimum-security wing. A smile was once again spread across his face and he jangled his foot to the Johnny Cash tune humming through his head. He thought about the bags packed at his feet, what the coming day would bring for him. A chance to leave. A chance to breathe again.

A prison guard stood in the hallway. The guard smiled at Douglas, a warm and kind visage the young kid had gotten used to. Most of the guards here liked Douglas—he was quiet and easy to talk to, didn't cause any trouble. And more often that not, his demeanor had a strong effect on the other inmates. Something about the way he spoke, or the way he listened, calmed the others. Some said the same thing about Cash during those concerts many years ago.

"Up and at 'em," the guard said, walking over to Douglas. "On your way, Dougie. And good luck."

Douglas stood and stretched out his legs. He had forsaken the prison oranges for his favorite denim shirt and black jeans—clothes for the real world. He grabbed his bag and followed the guard out of the cell, which held four other beds, and into the open hallway. Soon, orange suits were surrounding him, walking over with a smile and a handshake. Then a few more, then a few more, and soon Douglas was surrounded by most of the inmates in the block, coming to say good-bye to the popular kid in their unit. The one who was leaving. The one who got out.

As Douglas made his way through the sea of orange, one inmate started to clap and stomp his foot. Another soon followed. They began to pound out the opening rhythm to Queen's "We Will Rock You." No words, no humming, just the pounding of feet and hands, which reverberated across the metal-and-concrete ward.

Douglas walked across the open floor toward the exit. Queen? He would have preferred Cash, but most here were too young to remember the singer and what he once meant to this place. Douglas hadn't expected them to remember, but he hadn't expected this kind of farewell, either. He figured he might be the first man in the history of the prison to carry fond memories of the place with him out the door.

Douglas stopped just before the exit of the cell block and turned around. Most of the entire ward stood before him, stomping or clapping, projecting onto Douglas the joy they, too, would feel if they were able to leave. One day, one day soon.

Douglas cleared his throat to address the group, exhibiting his trademark killer smile.

"Whoa, whoa, whoa. I don't know why but . . .

I'm going to miss you guys," he said. The crowd fell silent for a moment. Then Douglas added, "For about five minutes!"

They all hooted and hollered at him, enjoying his final joke, as lame as it might be, all the more as he turned and walked out the door. No more good-bye needed.

Outside, Douglas walked free of the glass doors and down the concrete incline. He took a long, deep breath of freedom. Once again back in the real world, he could see the desert stretched out around him. The pale mountains and purple summit peaks, the dry heat glancing off his sculpted cheeks; he was eager for this. For the colors of the real world to come back to him.

He was just as eager when he saw the long pair of legs.

Douglas's sight was pulled from the desert landscape to the parking lot. Past the chain-link fences topped with barbwire sat a shiny red Mustang, glittering even in the dull morning light. Leaning on its hood was Allie. If not the girl of his dreams, then the girl of at least six or seven of them. Her long, eager legs ended in high, pointed heels that clicked as she ran across the blacktop to him.

"Baby . . ." She drew the word out to fill up the space between them. Her long, brown hair moved behind her as she picked up speed. Neither of them could wait. Their lips met first, open and hungry, just before she wrapped her long legs around his waist, crossing tattooed ankles at the small of his back.

Douglas grabbed her large, round ass and the backs of her thighs, keeping her wrapped around him, and walked them back toward the red Mustang. He dropped her on the hood of the car so he could get closer to her, nudging up closer and closer, their lips never pulling apart. It felt like he didn't need to breathe, not with her, not with both of them once again free in the real world.

Allie placed her hands on his backside and tried to move him even closer to her. Douglas felt the familiar stirring in his jeans as well as the heat radiating off her.

"I missed you," he said, finally coming up for air.

"Baby, before we wear the paint off the hood of my car, how 'bout we take this somewhere with a mattress?"

She looked like an angel but talked like a hooker, and to Douglas this combination was irresistible. She didn't have to ask him twice. He let go of her and ran to the other side of the car, throwing his bag in the backseat. They both jumped inside and Allie fired up the engine, its loud roar echoing across the empty lot.

Within a few seconds she was driving them away. Douglas took one last look at the prison, its large, imposing facade soon behind them as Allie drove the car toward the open road.

On the road leading away from the prison, Douglas grabbed a lollipop from the stash near the dashboard and popped it in his mouth. The sugar had almost the same effect as Allie, and he felt another rush straight to his head. Allie was focused on the road, her hair moving in the air from the open windows. Douglas breathed in the cool, rapid air.

Allie moved her hand from the wheel into her purse on the console and handed him a letter. It was a thin, white envelope with a red *special delivery* sticker.

"Oh, baby, this came for you today. Registered mail. Looked important."

Douglas took the letter from her. It felt light in his hand. He tore open the envelope, watching the desert pass by outside the window. The flat land seemed to lead in every direction, the two-lane road feeling like the only thing they needed to see it all. Orange mixed with reds and yellows, the sparse plant life bleached from the constant sun. So different from everything he had seen inside.

He pulled the letter out and held it up to read it. His eyes scanned the words and a slight, curious smile formed on his face. But that smile soon disappeared.

Allie noticed the change in his expression. A look of concern fell over her face. "Baby, what's the matter?"

Douglas tried to think of the words that might explain this to her. He didn't really understand it himself.

"My father's dead," he said.

Allie looked confused. She put her hand behind his head and started to massage his neck, which was now heavy and stiff.

"I thought you were an orphan?" she said.

Douglas tucked the letter back into its envelope and smiled.

"Even orphans have fathers," he said. "Somewhere."

And just like that, the new, real world lost some of its color.

Chapter
SIX

Finally making its way through the morning traffic, Wills's limousine pulled up to the curb of the school. The private Catholic school was tall and imposing, casting a long shadow across the wide street. Janson Wills grabbed his backpack, taking a few moments longer than needed to see if his dad would look up from the newspaper. It was a stupid trick, one he thought he had outgrown.

"Later, Dad," Janson said.

Janson slowly opened the door. Only when it shut, with its comfortable deep noise, did Wills look up from the paper. He glanced at the empty space beside him, the familiar sight of the school past the tinted window. He turned back to his paper, not noticing the large, blue truck that pulled up behind them in the traffic.

A few blocks away, a man sat at a bus stop reading the same newspaper. He was solid and wide, hard-looking but not unattractive, with slicked-back black hair and a thick goatee. As he read, his brow furrowed with an intense focus.

Next to him, Nicolas Canton was about to go apoplectic. A cell phone pressed hard against one ear, he felt his Hawaiian shirt begin to cling to his lower back with sweat. His face and neck were flushed a deep crimson.

Canton felt annoyed and preoccupied, keeping one eye on the strange, scary man beside him and the other on the bus lane.

"Ma, I don't care what your landlady said . . . What did the doctor . . . Ma." Canton's words went unheeded. His mother was already off on another subject. He hated talking to her in the morning, her least lucid time of day. He needed to find some money, fast. Her medical bills were piling up from the medications and specialists. Everyone seemed to have his hand out. Everybody wanted more than Canton could give.

Canton felt his patience end. "MA! WHAT DID THE DOCTOR SAY?" He couldn't control the volume of his voice any more than he could control her declining health. If only he hadn't lost his company. Canton often dwelled on the memory of how one billionaire businessman destroyed him and took his company. How the mogul brought in teams of lawyers and private investigators to dig and dig and dig for any scrap of dirty laundry. How the mogul distorted facts until even Canton's closest friends started to distance themselves from him. They even pulled up his mother's medical records, insinuating that not all of her medication was legally prescribed and that Canton dipped into the pills himself. All that pain and humiliation and loss of dignity and now he was left at a bus stop still trying to placate his sick mother.

Canton warily eyed Rodriguez, who kept his cool, letting his eyes travel up and down the street. Like a snake waiting to strike.

Behind him, a homeless woman pushing a shopping cart full of used blankets and stuffed animals hobbled by, emitting a distinct aroma of body odor and piss. Her unwashed hair formed a dirty cloud about her tired eyes, her grubby face. She walked up to Rodriguez with her dirty hand out.

"Any chance I could talk you out of a smoke?" she asked.

Rodriguez's dark eyes flashed with disgust. "No chance in hell. Walk away."

The woman took the hint and stepped back, once again taking up her cart and moving it down the street. Pushing her life through another day in sunny Los Angeles.

Barely noticing their interaction, Canton tried his best to focus on his mother's small, fragile voice. He hated losing his temper with her. But really, there was only so much a man could take.

"Look, I'm sorry, Ma," he said. His usual refrain when she felt she wasn't getting his full attention. But Canton had other things on his mind.

He looked down the street for the bus, then checked his watch once again. Traffic moved quickly on nearby Alameda Street, and Canton surveyed the long stretch of asphalt, looking for anything out of the ordinary. He felt his heart racing in his chest. Sweat continued to pour down his face. He wanted this to be over with quickly.

*   •   •

Just then a long, black limousine passed in front of the bus stop and stopped a few feet away from the men on the bench, coming to rest behind a cab at the traffic light. The limo was followed by a big, blue truck, which pulled up right behind it.

The light turned green, but the cab did not move. Traffic around them moved forward. Wills, sitting in the backseat, noticed the cars moving around him and turned his attention back to the paper. The limo driver sighed and tapped his horn, willing the cab to move.

Suddenly, the blue truck behind them roared forward, crashing into the limousine's back bumper. Wills and his bodyguard lurched from the impact. The cab, its tires squealing on the asphalt, went flying toward the limo in reverse, crashing into its front, pinning the limo in with nowhere to go. The hood bent and cracked.

Wills sensed panic forming in the limousine as both bodyguards grew alert, following the sounds of the collision. Wills's driver opened his door just as a pickup truck went speeding by, taking the door of the elegant car clean off its hinges. It bounced down the street, no longer looking so new and pristine. They were now surrounded by metal, trapped in the sleek, black prison.

"Jimmy, it's a hit!" yelled the bodyguard in the backseat. His large, meaty hand grabbed Wills's jacket. "Get on the floor," he commanded, throwing the startled businessman down into the carpeted footwells of the car. Wills's eyes grew wide when he saw the bodyguard draw his automatic weapon.

Their panic was punctured by the smooth, muffled sound of a bullet flying from the pickup truck right into the chest of the driver. A mist of blood flew out from him before he slumped over the wheel of the car, his life ended by one perfect shot.

Watching from the bus stop, Rodriguez pulled a ski mask over his face and drew his weapon, a high-powered handgun with a silencer attached. His black leather jacket hugged his body close as he moved toward the back of the limousine. He raised his weapon and fired multiple shots into the window. Tinted glass fell to the ground like marbles. One more shot, right to the head, killed the bodyguard instantly. His body slumped down on top of Wills, who was still pinned to the floor.

As people on the street ran screaming from the scene, the sounds of gunshots echoing through the air, a man exited the cab that had crashed into the front of the limo and drew his own weapon, the exact same model as the one Rodriguez had used to kill the bodyguard. He raised his arm and shot three bullets into the second bodyguard as he scrambled to exit the front seat. He went down like a sack of flour, his blood pooling in the concrete gutter and making a trail down the street.

Another man exited the back of the blue truck, ski mask hiding his face. He fired three gunshots into the air to increase the level of panic on the scene. He watched as people raced away from the street, hands covering their heads, everyone screaming and yelling, everyone eager to be as far away from the gunfire and the limo as possible. Leaving Wills alone and exposed.

The man walked quickly up to the limo, over the shattered glass now littering the street, and pulled the door open. Wills, looking like a wet kitten in the rain, cowered on the floor.

"Okay, okay," he said weakly, lifting his hands in surrender as if he knew the drill and had been waiting for this moment his entire life.

The man pulled Wills from the limo and led him to the back of the truck, all the while keeping the gun stuck in his back. Wills let out a whimper as the men who had rammed his limousine and killed his driver and two bodyguards in under one minute assembled and pulled open the truck doors, revealing a metal compartment, empty except for two benches. They forced Wills inside and soon followed suit, taking a seat on the bench opposite the frightened businessman. One man kept a gun at Wills's head the entire time. The last man bounded up into the back of the truck, Hawaiian shirt straining against his wide belly. He ripped off his ski mask and dropped it down on the bench beside his baggy shorts.

Canton surveyed the back of the truck and a laugh jumped from his mouth.

"Nicely done, boys. Let's giddyap!"

Wills shut his eyes, girding himself against the fast, jerking movements of the truck and the feel of the gun against his forehead. He tried not to think of the three dead bodies lying in their own blood. The horror of the scene. Who he would assign to tell their grieving families.

These men had come so quickly, taking him and his bodyguards by storm. Wills felt the deep fear growing in his stomach. He should have been more alert, more suspicious. Wills suspected he was about to pay a dear price for his inattention.

Chapter
SEVEN

The beautiful, austere church was one of the oldest in the area, its stone facade having held fast through several earthquakes, its red roof faded by the sun. It had become a place of great comfort for Nina, and she felt a sense of its power again as she walked toward the building, its tall, gold steeple and cross reaching out like a beacon against a blue sky empty of clouds.

The shock of the letters seemed to be keeping the boys on their best behavior. So far, so good. Sam arrived first, his expression blank as a sheet of paper. He said nothing as he hugged her, but she felt his love and support through the big bear hug.

Leo came next, letting the front door slam behind him, its loud echo reverberating across the entire church. There is no silence like that of a church, she thought, and hoped that its heaviness would keep them all in line, the stern, wagging finger of God making them behave. It worked when they were children, and she was counting on it to work now.

Leo hugged his sister quickly, gave a quick nod to Sam, and waited to see what else was going to happen.

Last to arrive was Douglas, whom Nina ushered into the pew next to her. Sam and Leo exchanged confused looks, which was expected, seeing as neither of them had ever laid eyes on the kid before.

A third brother—that was their first surprise.

Nina led the three men up to the front altar, where their father rested in the open casket. Nina sensed her brothers shifting impatiently. After a long silence, Sam gestured toward the wire-rimmed glasses that rested on their father's serene face.

"They expect him to do a lot of reading?" Leo asked. His voice echoed throughout the empty church.

44

"Leo, please . . ." Nina said. "The undertaker thought it made him look more natural."

She stared down at her father and began a silent prayer. She crossed herself and touched the pendant around her neck. Douglas, clearly at a loss for what to do, followed her lead but failed in his attempt, reversing the sign of the cross. Sam watched the young man, a stony look on his face.

"Could we let it go, at least for today?" Nina pleaded. "We're in God's house."

The three men quieted down. Almost.

"I can't read when I'm hot," Leo said. "Like by the pool out in Vegas? I don't know how they do it." He looked more closely at his father, his lifeless body before them. "We're talking Baghdad hot where you're going, old man."

"It's a dry heat," Sam added, smirking. Leo started to snicker.

"Will you please show some respect!" Nina yelled, louder than she meant to, not that it mattered in the big and empty church. There was no one there to watch them bicker or misbehave, with the possible exception of God Almighty. Suddenly, she felt like they were all children again. And her voice had the strict, severe tone of her mother.

But it worked. The three brothers fell deadly silent. Together, they shared a moment of peace and quiet.

Douglas spoke up next, in a voice hushed and respectful. "I need it quiet when I read. He should have plenty of that."

Leo laughed out loud, and Sam couldn't help but crack a smile himself.

"That was funny, kid," Leo said.

"It wasn't supposed to be funny," Douglas added, almost offended by the remark.

Leo and Sam both shot Douglas a strange look. *Who is this kid?*

"What was your name again?" Leo asked.

"Douglas," he replied.

Nina was once again near her breaking point, thinking of the day and the meeting that was to come. She felt angry all over again: angry at her dad for leaving her. Angry at what she had to do now, because of him.

"Listen to me, all of you," she began. "The man that lays here before us was a very different man in his final days. He changed a great deal for the good." She wondered why they couldn't see that. It was obvious to her that they didn't believe it.

"I can tell by the sell-out crowd," Sam said, motioning to the utterly empty church.

But Nina was on him, stepping between Sam and the casket. She'd had enough of this shit and went right up to his face. She met his eyes, the way she rarely did, and the anger came off her in waves. Sam almost took a step back, surprised at how fierce his little sister had become. Leo inched away, as did Douglas, as if they could watch this whole mess from a safe distance. As if they weren't a part of it.

"Well, then you're just going to have to take my word for it, Sam!" Her breath hit him square in the face. But she wasn't done. She turned to address all three of them. "Now, you'll all get your money in due time, but meanwhile, we stand here, quietly, and pay our respects to our father, *as a family*. Understood?"

The three men nodded solemnly, suddenly chastised. It was the first mention of the money—their sole purpose for being here today, Nina reminded herself. Her words had the intended effect but for the wrong reasons. To the three brothers, this wasn't about family. This was about money.

Nina stepped back to the casket and composed herself. This was stupid, she thought after a moment. *I'm sorry, Daddy. But I don't think we'll ever be a family again.*

Just then Nina felt movement behind her. Sam wrapped her tiny hand in his own and gave it a light squeeze, just like he used to. The familiar touch brought tears to her eyes. Following Sam's lead, Leo walked up beside Nina and grabbed her other hand, holding it gently but firmly. She felt comforted, as if her two brothers had truly returned to her.

Douglas, once again at a loss for what to do, fell in line next to Leo and reached for his hand. But Leo pulled it away quickly.

"Don't even think about it," he warned the kid.

Nina took a deep breath. She felt her brothers' solid presence around her. She held both hands tightly and wondered if her plan just might work after all.

Chapter
EIGHT

There was nothing in this part of the world as far as the eye could see. Sand, dirt, rocks, weeds. From out of this nothing came a single road, a simple tether back to the real world, that due south led to a swath of dead desert and pale rock formations, everything the same color, as if the relentless western sun had bleached it all clean. Dead and clean.

The single road eventually led to an abandoned compound, there in the middle of nowhere, that housed stone buildings, a group of huts with open verticals for eyes and guns. Pale green shrubs marked the perimeter of the area, seeking out what moisture they could from the occasional and sudden desert rains. Most of the indigenous people along this corridor of Mexico didn't like to come near it, fearing the area was haunted or cursed land because of the many bad things that had happened there. Americans had no such reservations. It was desolate, isolated, and didn't appear on any recent geographical maps. The perfect place to hide.

A modern satellite dish sat on the rooftop of one of the stone huts, the one closest to the outhouse. Various long-range radio antennae dotted the roof of the main building in the compound. A generator, set on a two-wheeled trailer, sat just outside the main house. Power cables ran off into other outbuildings. A stone cabin held a cot, a small kitchen, and two east-facing windows.

Four henchmen, of Indian and Mexican descent, casually walked the compound carrying automatic weapons. Even though they did not expect visitors, they were paid to stay on high alert, eager to shoot anything that approached.

A large wooden door, outfitted with modern locks, opened slowly. The door was made of wood planks reinforced with more wood, sturdy as hell, and not a crack of light came through its face.

Wills sat in the middle of this desolate cabin on a wooden cot covered only with an army-green blanket. A short wooden table rested near his shins. Two square windows were framed by gauzy curtains, the room's only source of air and light. If he closed his eyes, if he dreamed hard enough, he could almost imagine he was on vacation. That this rustic outpost was his wife's idea of getting away from it all. That she wanted her husband to spend quality time with their son away from the modern distractions of computer, phone, and television. But it didn't take long for that dream to become a nightmare.

An old Mexican woman entered the hut carrying a plate of cold rice, beans, tortillas, and some kind of meat. The food gave off no smell, and that made Wills even more wary of it. A few flies buzzed along the rim of the plate.

He sat on the edge of the cot, his legs shackled and connected to a steel eyebolt set into the stone floor. His hands were cuffed in front as well. He felt tired, still haunted by the sound of the gunfire in the limousine, the guards being shot right before his eyes, the strange bloom of red mist that sprang from his driver's chest before he went down. His clothes were stained and torn. He figured some of that mist must have gotten on him, and he felt dirty and shrouded in that sense of death.

The old woman set the food down on the small table in front of him. She poured him a glass of questionable water from a nearby pitcher. Wills searched her face for some glimpse of kindness or compassion. He could find neither. But if Kyle Wills had learned anything during his career, it was that every person had a price.

"Please," he said to her. "Please . . . how much money for you to help me?"

The woman just looked at him. Her eyes were cloudy pitchers of milk.

"Do you understand?" he asked in a whisper. "*Habla* English?"

The old woman nodded slowly. She didn't seem afraid of him and he took this as a good sign. She would help him, he hoped. She would help him and then he would give her all the money she wanted.

"Anything you want," he continued, urging his eyes to look kind and convincing. "Anything in this world . . . if you help me."

The old woman stopped nodding. Her face, framed by long, dark hair, was as rough hewn as the rock structures that surrounded the compound. Her expression was impassive.

Wills stared into her eyes pleadingly, willing her to speak her demands. He could buy her off. Kyle Wills could buy anyone off.

She opened her mouth to speak. "Can you buy me a place in Heaven?" she asked. A smirk grew upon her weathered old face, one that exposed her missing teeth.

She walked back out the door, making a noise to herself, laughter or some other kind of scathing music. She shut the heavy door behind her, and Wills was left alone once again.

"Wait," he said. But she was already gone. He slumped over on his cot, his body giving in to the hopelessness he felt inside. There was no one to help him.

Chapter
NINE

Everything in the lawyer's office was beige: the carpet, the walls, the file folders. Nina had been there before, but only today did she notice the drab interior, how the green tree in the corner was the only thing in the room to offset all the beige. It struck her as depressing, and it made her feel more nervous than she already was.

The lawyer sat behind his desk holding a copy of her father's will. Leo, Sam, and Douglas, she noticed, sat as far apart from one another as the small space allowed. Leo finally gave up and started pacing the back of the room like a chicken looking for seed.

"Your father's will reads pretty standard," the

lawyer began, keeping his eyes locked on Nina. She shifted uncomfortably in her seat. "After a lot of legal mumbo jumbo, that boils down to about three million dollars." He paused. "Apiece."

The room became as silent as a church. Nina couldn't take a breath, waiting for the other shoe to drop. She could feel the energy coming off her brothers. It was like someone had just thrown raw meat to a den of hungry lions. She stared intensely at the lawyer.

"What?" Leo asked, as if he had just invented the word.

"Three million each," the lawyer continued. No one in the room noticed Nina nodding slightly.

Sam held perfectly still, heavy and unmoving. Douglas, once again, looked like he didn't know what to do or say. Which left it up to Leo.

"Oh *my God,*" Leo screamed, sudden joy and disbelief spreading across the lines of his face. He raised his fists triumphantly.

"I'm free at last, thank you, Lord Almighty. I'm free at last!"

Nina observed that Sam had retained his usual stoic composure. She knew the sheer amount of money wasn't lost on him, but, always the cop, he still looked skeptical.

"Jesus. I figured 'substantial estate' meant a two-bedroom condo in Boca," Sam said. *Three million dollars. Each?* he thought. He could pay off his alimony, send his kids to college, and not ever have to worry about getting suspended from the force again.

Douglas watched his new brothers' reactions with unexpected glee. They seemed like kids in a candy store, which, he guessed, they were. They all were. A few days ago, Douglas was an orphaned inmate with no road toward the future. And now this. A huge smile cracked over his face.

"A family and money at the same time?" Douglas said, shaking his head.

Leo marched in between his seated brothers and clapped his palms on the lawyer's wide oak desk. "What'd the old man do?" he asked excitedly. "Did he rob a bank or something?"

"As it turns out, his fifth wife was pretty well-off," the lawyer said calmly.

"Was she sucking a tailpipe when he proposed to her?" Leo asked.

Nina blanched. "Leo, please. She loved him very much until the day she died."

Sam couldn't help himself. "I'll bet the old man's prints were all over that one."

But Nina wasn't going to listen to it. "Good Lord, stop! Daddy left us this money, that's the bottom line." She waited to make sure she had each brother's attention. She wanted them to listen very carefully. "But there are some . . . contingencies."

Leo stopped dead in his tracks, and suddenly all eyes were on Nina. She felt her pulse quicken.

"What—what are you talking about?" he asked his sister. "It's in pesos?"

The lawyer looked at Nina knowingly and rose from his chair. He looked uncomfortable.

"Listen. How about I get a cup of joe and you kids sort this out." He gathered up his suit jacket and quickly departed, letting the door shut briskly behind him.

Nina watched him leave and then took a breath. "First of all, Daddy left me as the executor of the estate."

The three men looked at one another. So far, no problem.

"That seems to make a lot of sense," Leo said, taking the chair the lawyer had vacated. "Somebody we all trust."

"Yeah," Sam interjected, "because if we give the money to Leo, he'll piss it away."

Leo bristled behind the big desk. "Look, I know you think you're this big, mature man, but I run a business, okay? I'm a businessman."

Before he could get too wound up, Nina jumped in.

"There's more," she said.

"Okay?" Leo said, eager for her to be out with it. Nina knew her brother hated surprises, most bail bondsmen did, and he definitely seemed to feel one coming.

She addressed the boys. "You will get the money if you work together in a *family business* for two years."

Silence once again fell over the room.

There were a few long beats of breathing as Nina waited for her brothers' reactions, studying each of their faces for a sign of what they were thinking. She knew she was in untested waters. She had no idea what to expect, what they might do. But she had gone too far to turn back now.

Douglas was the first to speak. His face was open and smiling. "Easy," he said.

Leo stared at his sister as if he didn't know what to say, as if, for once, all language had left him.

Sam's face was calm and reserved, as rigid as always. But his neck appeared to have doubled in size. He clapped his hands on his thighs and stood up from his chair.

"Douglas, right?" he asked, pointing at the kid.

"Yeah," Douglas said, bright and eager, like a puppy.

"Nice knowing ya, kid, have a good life."

With that, Sam headed for the door. Nina swore the room shook as he passed her.

"Sam, wait," she said, going after him.

"You know, Nina," Leo said from behind the lawyer's desk, "I love you very much, Nina, but this is not funny." He jumped up from the chair to follow her and Sam out the door.

Douglas, once again following the others, yelled out after them. "Hey, what about a deli?"

Sam marched down the street with a fast stride, heading for his car. After a moment, Nina, followed by Leo and then Douglas, all went bursting through the door in pursuit of their oldest brother. But Sam didn't break his stride, and Nina ran to catch up with him.

"It was his *dying wish* to bring us back together as a family!" she yelled. "*His dying wish!* Doesn't that mean anything to you, Sam?"

Sam stopped in his tracks a few paces away and turned to her.

"What are the three of us going to do together for two years without killing each other?" he asked.

Leo and Douglas caught up to them. Leo stepped in front of Nina and made a beeline for Sam's face.

"You know what your problem is, Sam?"

"Oh, I got plenty of ideas," he said, looking at his brother.

Nina ran to them, afraid a fight might break out. This wasn't the way it was supposed to turn out.

"You're not a 'glass half empty' kind of guy," Leo said. "You're a 'shove the glass up your ass' kind of guy. You figured this wasn't going to work before you walked in the door!"

Sam tried to control the anger in his voice, to no avail. "This is what I love about family. We haven't seen each other in over ten years, yet we can pick up and hate each other like it was yesterday."

"Sam, stop it," Nina pleaded. She was now afraid for all of them. One punch thrown and everything would fall apart. Her father's dying wish would die along with him.

"That reminds me," Leo said, pointing a finger at his sister. "Just because junior here is supposedly the old man's seed, doesn't mean he earned his fair share. He never even met the bastard."

Now Douglas was drawn into the fight and was obviously insulted by Leo's words.

"He's Daddy's son and your half brother, and I have the documents to prove it," Nina said, trying to regain control of the situation. She had come too far to let it all fall to shit now. "You all need this money . . . desperately." She turned to Sam. "You have alimony, you have college tuitions up the road, you are suspended without pay."

She turned to Leo. "And you. A bail bonds-man? Really?"

"What?" Leo countered. "I provide a service to the community."

"Yeah," she said. "In hock up to your eyeballs."

Finally she turned to Douglas. He looked so young standing there in the shadow of his two older brothers. "And you, a thief!"

Sam and Leo blanched—more information about the kid.

"I'm a good thief. Like Brad Pitt in *Ocean's Eleven*."

"I'll be sure and rent the DVD, thank you." She took a deep breath and continued on as forcefully as she could. "Now, I'm not saying you don't have good reason for what's become of you. But this is a blessing—this is a second chance for us to be a family. That was his dying wish and you will honor it even if it kills you."

Less than thirty minutes had passed since Nina's tirade, and the three brothers slunk into a nearby bar to nurse their thoughts. Sam had never seen his sister so angry and her outburst gave him pause, if only because it was so rare. Something about this arrangement was fishy, he could feel it. Every cop instinct he had told him so.

He drank his beer slowly, ignoring the two brothers at his side, and his eyes traveled up to the television hanging over the bar. He pretended to watch the game, oblivious to the others around him.

A breaking news story interrupted the game and suddenly a blond anchor filled the screen. She spoke urgently about a local kidnapping.

"We interrupt this broadcast for a special report. Billionaire businessman Kyle Wills was kidnapped today while en route to his office. Eyewitness reports from shocked onlookers described a chaotic scene in which . . ."

Sam took another sip of his beer and stared down at the bottle. More crime in the city, and there was nothing he could do about it. Suspended cops don't get to go after kidnapped businessmen. He bet Captain Haymer was shitting bricks right about now—a high-profile kidnapping done right on the streets of downtown was the last thing the department needed. The mayor would be breathing down all of their necks over this one. So much for the new-and-improved, sensitive LAPD.

Douglas sat between Sam and Leo, almost glad for the company, even with all the tension between them. Now that the game was off, he did his best to try and make conversation.

"So, what was it like growing up together, guys?" he asked.

They both looked at him as if he had just sprouted a second head.

"C'mon," he prodded, eager for some history or knowledge of his two new brothers. "I grew up in child facilities and foster homes but we still had a good time."

Leo, already on his third beer, decided to take the bait, only because he couldn't put a bullet in the kid.

"You wanna know what it was like?" Leo said. "I'll give you a taste. You ever play the game 'got-cha last'?"

Sam groaned and went back to his drink. *Here we go again,* he thought. If Leo held on to a bail bond the way he held on to a grudge, he'd be a millionaire.

"No . . ." said Douglas, now afraid of where this was going

"Oh," Leo said sarcastically, "it's great. What you do is you hit each other back and forth—*boom, boom, boom*—one guy gets the other guy really good. Then you run away and say 'Gotcha last.' Then the other guy chases after you and tries to hit you back and it starts all over again. It's kinda fun. Except when you play it with Sam."

Douglas grew hesitant, already knowing he'd accidentally opened up a can of worms. But Leo was on a tear, and he wasn't going to back down.

"You know what Sam would do? I'd finally get Sammy good, then I'd run off. But he wouldn't chase after me. And I would live in fear for hours, sometimes even days, wondering when the big, bad Sam was going to attack me." Leo paused to take a big swig of beer. "And you know what your brother from another mother would do?"

Leo gulped down the last of the beer, upending the bottle angrily. "He would set his alarm for three a.m. and walk into my room when I was sound asleep and slap the shit out of me! And I'd be laying there looking up at this monster, and he'd lean down and say, 'Gotcha last.' And that was the *funnest* game we played. The rest I keep between myself and my therapist."

"Grow up," Sam said, getting up from the bar stool. He'd had enough. He'd heard this all before.

"Kiss my ass, Sam!" Leo yelled.

Sam opened his wallet and put a few bucks down on the bar. He patted Douglas on the shoulder as a form of good-bye, then walked behind him to an unsuspecting Leo. Before his brother could move, Sam punched Leo with a hard right cross, knocking him off the stool. Leo, stunned, looked back up at his brother towering over him.

Sam looked down at him and said, "Gotcha last."

With that, Sam turned and walked out of the bar.

Leo scrambled to his feet, holding his jaw and wincing in pain. Douglas reached out to help him stand, but he pushed the kid away, intent on pursuing Sam. Then Leo stopped dead in his tracks, his eyes moving from Sam's exit to the television screen above the bar.

Larger than life, flashing on the television, was a mug shot of Edgar Rodriguez. The reporter continued:

"A homeless woman at the scene of the kidnapping identified this man, Edgar Rodriguez, as one of the Wills kidnappers. According to the FBI, Rodriguez is an escaped fugitive facing charges for grand theft and assault with a deadly weapon."

Leo could not believe it. "Rodriguez!" he yelled to Douglas, to the bartender, to anyone who would listen. "That's my bail skip!"

"The Wills family is offering a five-million-dollar reward for any information directly resulting in the billionaire's safe return."

As the TV reporter continued, Leo stared at the face of Edgar Rodriguez. First the will and now this. He wondered how he was ever going to put his life back together again.

Chapter
TEN

The man named Nealon was, once upon a time, an average gun for hire, a Los Angeles–based mercenary with a mean streak, nicknamed the Iceman since he often killed his marks at close range and in cold blood. Then he developed a penchant for prescription drugs. So it didn't take long for him to become involved with the Mexican cartels, seeing as he was in Tijuana most weekends stocking up on farm-grade tranquilizers, human growth hormones, Valium, and any other body-altering substance he might be able to pawn off on the less-demanding users across lower downtown and the east side of Los Angeles. The pills were easy enough to hide from border patrol, his customers less than discerning if he kept the price right, which given the sorry state of the peso, was easy enough to do. But years of running pills and helping the gym rats of LA get juiced up soon grew boring, if not mildly profitable, and Nealon wanted more. It was then he learned about something new to sell, something infinitely more valuable than pills or steroids: freedom. The kidnapping game in Mexico exploded almost overnight, and it was there Nealon realized the true way to money and power was to sell something that was already protected and valued: a human life. One meeting led to another and soon Nealon was allied with Edgar Rodriguez, the meanest son of a bitch south of the border. By that time, Americans had grown wise to the workings down south and it became difficult to entice any of them to Mexico, regardless of what security was arranged and promised. So Nealon decided they needed to go fishing. If the rich businessmen were not going to travel to Mexico for fear of being kidnapped, Nealon would have to go find them. And he wanted to start with the biggest fish in the pond: LA billionaire Kyle Wills.

Their target sat chained to the floor in the stone

cabin, lost in thought, roughed up and bruised from the abduction. Nealon pushed through the heavy wooden door, ignoring the rich man stuck on the bed, followed closely by Canton and his laptop. Nealon was rooting around in his green pack, looking for something that would help take the edge off for their "houseguest" but still leave him coherent enough to be presentable. The trick, he knew, for getting the best price was to leave the victim calm and weary, yet still obviously vulnerable. With Wills they had nothing to worry about. The man looked ready to shit himself, if he hadn't already.

Nealon pulled out an unmarked prescription bottle and crossed over to Wills. He shook one blue pill into the palm of his hand and handed it to Wills.

"Take this," he said. "Ten mills of Valium. You'll think you're at Club Med."

Wills took the pill but inched back a bit. Nealon smelled of smoke and body odor, his voice gravelly and rough.

"I don't need this," Wills said meekly.

Nealon handed him a ceramic cup filled with water. "I'm doing you a favor. Take it or I'll shove it down your throat."

Wills put the pill in his mouth and chased it with some water. It went down easily enough.

Canton pulled out his laptop and set it up on the wooden table in front of Wills. The man looked familiar to Wills somehow, and certainly didn't seem like the rest of his captors. Educated, somewhat clean, sporting a Hawaiian shirt when the others favored denim or combat fatigues. He was the one who stuck out, the one who didn't belong. Wills wondered how he might be able to exploit that.

"Okay, all of our communications with the FBI are done through computer. Very high-tech. You wouldn't understand—you're only good at destroying computer companies. You don't know jack shit about how to use one."

Wills just stared at him. He couldn't argue that point.

"May I talk with my family somehow?" he asked.

"Will you please shut up! You think I'm some kind of ogre?" Canton said, turning the laptop around so that it faced Wills. "You see that camera? What do you think I bought that for? They see you, you see them, everybody cries and begs for mercy, et cetera, et cetera."

Wills looked down at the laptop. He could just make out his reflection in the monitor's screen. He looked beaten. Defeated.

Canton whipped the computer back around and began typing on the keypad before placing it back in front of Wills. "Now, the Feds are gonna wanna make sure you're alive, so I've rigged a live feed of the Dow Jones stock ticker to run on the bottom of the screen. That way, you can read real-time stock quotes and see just how far your company's gone down the toilet because their faithful leader is about to die a horrible death unless they pay up. Cool, huh?"

Wills looked at the man with barely disguised disdain. But he held his tongue, not knowing what else to do.

Nealon stood in the corner watching his prey. The man was smart. He was going to play along. That would keep him alive. And make Nealon a very rich man.

He watched Canton work his magic and the keypad, and soon the feed went live. Wills began to read the stock ticker, his voice calm and even, the Valium having its intended effect.

Wills read the numbers along the bottom of the screen as his wife and son appeared on the monitor. *Dow's down forty-four, S&P's down four, NASDAQ up sixteen . . .*

His wife looked so scared. Usually she was so bright, so well put together. In the few instances when he took the time to notice, she looked beautiful, not that different from the woman he met decades ago. But here, on the monitor, she looked older, obviously having had little sleep. Her trembling hand rested on Janson's shoulder.

Volume's light, six hundred thirty million shares . . .

And his son—he was growing up so fast. So eager to learn about his father's world, yet there were so many things Wills had to keep from him. From them both. He had to reach out to them. The pill had dulled his words but not the feelings underneath them. He had to do something.

"Susan, Janson," he said as quickly as the Valium would let him. "I'm okay. Janson, I want . . ."

But the signal was cut. They were gone. Wills was left looking at a blank and dark screen. At his own failed reflection.

Chapter
ELEVEN

The square brick colonial had been Nina's for years, the product of a successful divorce, good timing in the real estate market, and a small gift from her father's equally small estate. It contained three cozy bedrooms, one bathroom, and a plush lawn with two trimmed trees standing sentry in the front yard. The perfect place to raise a family, should she ever get around to doing so. At present it housed only her and her three brothers, all of whom were now sitting hungrily around the breakfast table. Funny how the one thing they had in common—hunger— quieted their constant bickering, at least long enough for her to fix some eggs and make some toast. After that, it was anybody's guess.

The three brothers ate silently, or as silently as they could, shoving the food into their mouths. They ignored one another until Nina looked over at Leo, who nodded in her direction. She got the hint and braced for impact.

"Okay," she said quickly. "Leo needs a favor."

Sam and Douglas seemed not to hear her and continued to attack their breakfast. Leo, feeling earnest and contrite, with a bruised jaw from Sam's surprise punch at the bar, took this as a good sign and barreled forward. He didn't want to let on how badly he needed their help. How desperate he truly was.

"Yeah, yeah . . . see, I was thinking that until we figure out whatever it is we're going to do together in the 'family business,' I've got a situation I could use a little help with."

Sam took a deep breath but kept his head down. But Douglas, ever the eager puppy, piped up first.

"How can I help, bro?"

Leo looked over at him, annoyed. He needed their help, but he just couldn't stop himself. "Bro? What are you, twelve years old? Next you're gonna be asking me to high-five you."

Nina, losing her patience, stepped in before

Leo blew the whole thing. "Do you want help or don't you, Leo? Beggars can't be choosers."

Leo knew she was right, as always. "Right, right, sorry." He regained his earnest demeanor and continued on. "Well, turns out I won't be getting the old man's cut for two years and I'm in a little bit of a financial bind. I posted this bond on this guy Edgar Rodriguez for two hundred fifty thousand dollars, and he skipped on me. And if he doesn't show up for his trial next week, I'm on the hook for the two hundred fifty thousand dollars."

Sam stared down at his plate and rubbed his temples. "This is a nightmare," he said under his breath.

Leo, misinterpreting Sam's comment for sympathy, quickly added, "I know, tell me about it."

At this point, Sam's eyes started to bore a hole in Leo's forehead, but his brother didn't seem to notice. "But the good news," he continued, "is it seems that Rodriguez is involved with that Kyle Wills kidnapping that's all over the news. So we got that going for us."

Sam shook his head at his younger brother's naïveté. A skipped bond worth two hundred and fifty grand that was now in the middle of a major federal investigation into the kidnapping of a prominent American billionaire? To him it was almost comical how clueless Leo was, even to the details of his own business. It was no wonder he was in hock up to his eyeballs. There was no way Sam was having any part of this—and certainly no way any sort of family business would ever work out.

Sam's mind still hadn't cleared hours later when Nina convinced him to take a walk in a nearby park. It was one of her favorite things to do, dating back to when they were kids. She used to beg Sam to take her to the park, to her favorite swing in the middle of the sandlot. Sam, already big and strong for his age, would push her as high and as fast as she wanted to go. It was one of his favorite memories from his childhood—one of his *only* memories from that time that he could stomach remembering.

The day was breezy and bright as they made their way down the slope of grass. Sam watched the other people in the park go by—good parents playing with good children, throwing a ball or Frisbee, playing a harmless game of tag where one touch wouldn't lead to a fistfight, no one screaming "Gotcha last" with bruises on their arms or bloodied noses. Nina grabbed his arm and pulled him near her, as if she could sense the memories were close around him.

"The old man's probably laughing his ass off. You know that was his plan all along."

"No it wasn't," Nina said, dropping his arm. "He knew it would take that long. Especially you, Sammy the Bullheaded. Just like him."

The comparison stopped Sam dead in his tracks. She couldn't have meant it. Still, it stung.

"You're the only one on this planet I would let compare me to him. I want you to know that."

Nina laughed. "What would you do? Slap me around like one of your perps? Now, wouldn't that bring down the wrath of God, huh?"

Her levity was a bit infectious and Sam smiled himself. "You should've been a nun."

Now it was Nina's turn to laugh at herself. "Yeah—cheated on my husband, ruined my marriage, and excommunicated from the Church."

Even Sam had to agree that his sister's actions would be tough for the Church to swallow. But he was hardly one to cast judgment, and he told her so. "I got two failed marriages and a kid who barely knows me. I'm damned to hell for sure. Chips off the old block, eh?" he said. Perhaps they weren't that different from the old man after all. The thought almost made him wince.

"Bullshit, Sammy. It's time you grew up and just stopped blaming him. Now it's up to us."

Her words were not lost on him, and he pulled her close once again. She could always have this effect on him. Helping him see the larger picture.

Nina noticed the change in her brother's demeanor and saw her chance to convince him.

"I love my brothers," she said. "Unconditionally. Even you. Even the one I just met."

Sam laughed once again. "Really? What's his name?"

"Douglas," she said, not missing a beat. "He seems very sweet."

"For a juvenile delinquent," Sam added.

"Yeah, well . . . you're no prince, either, but I still love you. . . . That's kind of how family works, Sammy."

Her words lingered in the afternoon air. Sam knew she was trying hard to do the right thing, what she thought was best for her and for her family. Even that word made him cringe. There was nothing traditional about their family, thanks to the old man. He had been the worst father figure imaginable: the multiple wives, the drinking, the outbursts. But he was gone, dead and buried, and Sam agreed with Nina that what happened from here on out was up to them.

Maybe things could be different. Maybe something good could come from the old man after all—something besides the large amount of money.

And there, in the middle of the park, Sam knew he was going to help Leo out after all.

Chapter
TWELVE

The next day, Sam gathered Leo and Douglas at the local bar. Sam sat them at a table and actually paid for the first round of beers. So Leo was on high alert, while Douglas was just thirsty.

Leo remained a bit guarded until he actually heard the words coming out of Sam's mouth. He was stunned but, in his usual style, not speechless.

"You're actually going to help me out?" Leo asked.

"The FBI will throw every agent they have at this thing. Wills is a big contributor to the Republican Party. They're going to find Rodriguez before we do."

"Yeah, except they won't be looking for Rodriguez, not just yet. Look, they know this guy's not smart enough to pull off something this big. He's nothing but a lieutenant with the cartels down in Mexico."

"So we interfere with an FBI investigation and get killed by the cartels?"

"Yeah, but there's a five-million-dollar reward," Douglas added.

"We're not looking for Wills, so there is no five million," Leo said.

"So we split your bond. That's what, ten percent on two hundred and fifty K? Twenty-five grand split three ways is eight thousand, three hundred and thirty-three and change so . . ."

"Listen, Einstein, the deal was we work together and split the old man's money. That bond is mine."

"No," Sam interjected. "This counts as part of our two-year sentence, and the deal was whatever the company makes along the way is split three ways. That's the deal."

A long pause fell across the table. Sam knew that Leo had no choice but to accept his terms. He needed the help, and no one else was stepping forward for the job. Sam knew this. And so Leo relented.

"Tell me what you know about Rodriguez," Sam said.

"Slow down, Turbo," Leo said defensively. He was the expert, and he should take the lead. "I can see how things are going here. You're snapping out orders and expecting the two of us to just eat shit. No. Nina said we work together as a team."

"Oh, well, thank you, John Wooden," Sam said, getting angry at Leo's ungrateful attitude. "I'm a cop, that's what I do. Along the way I'll try to figure out what contribution you make to the team. Until then I'm stumped."

Leo stared hard at Sam's imposing figure.

"Listen, Rodriguez was always running his mouth off about this girl he was dating, some famous stripper down in Mexico City."

Sam shook his head in dismay. It just kept getting worse. A federal kidnapping investigation, Mexican cartels, and now strippers? Mexico City was a hotbed of criminal activity. Every cop in the city and outer regions was corrupt and somehow on the take, either from the cartels or some other criminal with enough cash to pay a bribe.

"You know how many strip clubs there are in Mexico City?" he said.

"She's famous, right?" Douglas added, trying to be helpful. "That narrows it down."

"Angelina. Angelina. That was her name. It was a singular name. Like Madonna."

Sam just looked at them both. They were doomed before they'd even started. Some American running around town asking for a stripper with a name similar to Madonna's was just asking to get shot.

"Just hear me out, okay?" Leo said. "If Rodriguez is involved, he's involved because of his connections to the cartels in Mexico. So it's my guess that that's where they're hiding Wills."

Sam tried to follow his brother's logic, but it remained cloudy. He didn't see how one unknown stripper would lead them to Rodriguez, who in turn would lead them to the kidnapped billionaire. But it was all they had. And they'd have to make do with that.

"We're going to need money to get started," Sam finally said. And if they needed money, they needed to talk to Nina.

• • •

Later that night at Nina's house, Sam waited to speak to her when she was alone. He sat patiently while she puttered around the kitchen. She stood in the hallway dragging a spoon through a bowl of ice cream when she noticed him sitting alone at the table. The look on his face said everything.

"So how much do you need?" she asked.

"Fifteen thousand," Sam said. "That should get us started. I'll call you if we need more."

The number seemed to give her pause. "Fifteen grand," she said. Another long, thoughtful pause. "Well . . . I plan on running a tight ship, Sam. I don't plan on dipping into Daddy's funds until you've all proved yourself a bit." She joined him at the table, watching the ice cream melt in the bowl. Trying to act responsible. "So ten thousand will have to do. No more."

"You're being a little tight with twelve million, don't you think?" he asked. Clearly Sam hadn't anticipated this little hoop his sister was asking him to hop through and was annoyed at best.

"It's not our money yet," she countered. "The company needs to prove itself; it has to be successful. I think ten thousand seems fair."

Annoying, yes, but then again, she was the boss and one of the few people on this earth that Sam had any respect for. "Okay. You're holding the purse strings. We'll see how it goes." Sam got up from his chair, intent on starting to pack. He wanted to leave early in the morning.

"You'll be careful, won't you, Sam? You'll look out for them?"

"They're grown-ups, Nina. I'll do my job. I'm not a babysitter."

"No. But they are your family."

"I'd keep pushing the money angle if I were you, kid. I'll see you in a week."

Sam left the room, his footsteps falling heavily on the wood floor and down the hallway, leaving Nina alone at the table. Her mind was racing with all the things that could go wrong. With the entire idea of money. Let alone what kind of trouble her brothers were about to get themselves into.

"Shit," she said, barely audible in the now-empty room.

Chapter
THIRTEEN

The flight to Mexico City took hardly any time at all. They were armed with the ten grand from Nina but little in the way of plans to find Edgar Rodriguez. Sam knew they had to come up with a more concrete way to find Rodriguez, but he remained quiet and stoic, drifting back into cop mode, eager to find the perp. His recent suspension still weighed heavily on his mind, and he was almost glad to have the distraction of Leo's skipped bail to deal with. But that was one thing he knew he could always count on with Leo: there was always some problem that needed fixing.

Leo sat near the window of the plane, finally quiet for once, nervous about the amount of money he'd have to produce should they not find Rodriguez. His entire business, his entire future, rested on this trip having a success-ful outcome. He hated to admit how much he needed his brother's help. He hated knowing that Sam was one of the only people who could help him out of this jam. But knowing Sam knew was what bothered him the most.

Only Douglas seemed upbeat, happy in the act of travel and spending time with the two brothers he never knew he had. He talked to the flight attendant, and even managed to get a free beer or two, which he tried to share with Leo, who rebuffed him once again.

They made their way through the Mexico City airport as quickly as they could and hailed down the least dilapidated cab they could find. It smelled of onions and sweat. Soon they were on their way downtown, the three brothers crowded into the backseat of the taxi.

From what Douglas could see from the cab window, the city was not that different from downtown LA, just more extreme: more smog, more traffic, more people. And more color, too. He spied an ancient cathedral drenched in years of dirt, a colorful fruit stand near a traffic light, and a gang of children running down the street, boxes of chewing gum in their hands. He chewed on a toothpick, glad to see it all. Glad to still be a part of the real world.

Douglas was already getting used to the way his two new brothers bickered back and forth. Sam was tough, Douglas could see that, and he also was usually right. And Leo—well, he was hapless, but he did have a charm about him that reminded Douglas of a few of the friendly inmates back at Folsom.

"So, Sam," he asked, "what's first?"

But Leo jumped in to answer instead, not wanting to let Sam be the leader of their mission. "I say we take a little nap and then hit the strip clubs. Pretty much my normal routine in any new town," he said, grinning.

"No," Sam said. "We call every club in town and ask if they've got a famous stripper named Angelina. Should take about a lifetime." He once again looked at Leo with disdain.

Douglas continued to be fascinated by the city and the busy streets and leaned toward the window. There, plastered against the brick facade of a passing building, was a huge billboard extolling the home of the greatest stripper in Mexico

City. One word was written across the top: *Angelina*. A picture of her beautiful face and generous assets blocked the entire horizon, a sexy punch of color against the drab bricks that made up the building.

Douglas's eyes almost fell out of his head. "It might not take as long as you think."

All three brothers leaned toward the window. Bricks never had it so good.

The three brothers arrived at the strip club after a short drive in their rental car, a dusty Jeep that had seen better days. The space was standard strip-club fare—one large stage in the center of the room, with four satellite stages surrounding it, smelling of strong perfume and, faintly, of pine disinfectant. Around the perimeter of the room was one long, continuous bar, most likely with good tequila for the locals and watered-down piss for the gringos. Strippers danced on the smaller stages, but the large center stage was kept empty, waiting for its star, Angelina.

Red light permeated the smoke-filled room. Within a few minutes, thanks to a large handful of American dollars, the three brothers were sitting at a table with Angelina. The billboard didn't lie. She was gorgeous, a comic book drawing come to life: long, dark hair, rich red lips, voluptuous breasts barely contained by her small negligee and corset. The upper shelf of her left breast sported a small, dark tattoo. Her long legs could cross the border from here, if she wanted to. Instead, she tucked them seductively under the table.

Leo and Douglas had a hard time concentrating on the task of finding Rodriguez, obviously smitten with her breathtaking beauty. But Sam, in cop mode, kept a wary eye out, noticing the angry glares of the few patrons of the club, especially two surly types throwing back beer and tequila at the long, wooden bar. They talked among themselves, but the music was too loud for Sam to hear them, even if he could speak Spanish, which he could not. But he didn't need a translator to understand the expressions on their faces. If their looks could kill, Sam and his brothers would soon have been heading back to Nina's place in three body bags.

José and Fillipe eyed the lousy Americans with open hatred and disdain. Flashing their American dollars and taking up the precious time of their beloved Angelina. José was large, like a sumo wrestler or a bull, angry and very drunk. Fillipe was the mouse on his shoulder, slender and just as nasty. And just as drunk.

"Look at those gringos with Angelina," José said in Spanish. *"It makes me puke that they are close enough for my angel to smell their foul breath."*

Fillipe looked over his shoulder, then back to his friend. He, too, felt his anger rising and searched for a way to express his love for the beautiful stripper. *"I would cut off my manhood and present it to her as a trophy of my love if only she would grace me with her beautiful smile,"* he said in Spanish.

José nodded in agreement. *"She told me she wants me,"* José said, rubbing his hands across his very large belly.

Fillipe compared the size of the wonderful Angelina to that of his drunk friend. *"You sure, José?"* he asked. *"I mean, no offense, but you're a big, fat, ugly man, and she is truly God's most beautiful and greatest gift."*

"What are you saying?" José slurred. Everyone knows opposites attract.

94

* * *

Back at the table, Leo and Douglas were just as entranced by Angelina. The red light of the club seemed to enhance her beauty. Her eyes were vivid and round. Her voice was clear, even if her English was not.

"Edgar is a very dangerous man," she said. "He would easily kill me if he thought I was a help to you. I have not seen him since he left for America over a month ago."

Her face was sincere but her body did not follow. Under the table, she slid off one patent-leather stiletto, letting the air hit her toes, delicately wrapped in fishnet stockings. She stretched her long leg over to Douglas's lap, sliding her curved foot near the inside of his thigh. Douglas felt a jolt of electricity, a thrill in his Levi's. He tried not to let it show on his face, but she knew exactly what she was doing to him.

Leo, oblivious to her flirtation with Douglas, tried to sway her attention in his direction. "Listen, Angelina, you don't have to be afraid of him anymore, okay?" he said, playing the big man. "We can protect you."

But Sam jumped in, annoyed at his brother's

false bravado. "No, we can't, Leo. Don't offer anything you can't deliver."

Angelina remained nonplussed. Her attentions were directed elsewhere. "It wouldn't matter. I can't help you. I'm sorry."

The emphasis on the words *I'm sorry* caused Angelina to rub her foot harder, reaching her delicate limb up into the sweet spot of Douglas's lap. He smiled and let his head fall back, a small sound escaping his mouth. The action was subtle but noticed by José and Fillipe at the bar, who from their vantage point could see the beautiful stripper's leg extended underneath the table. José had seen enough. He staggered to his feet and made a beeline for the table, despite Fillipe's attempt to hold him back.

Linebacker, sumo wrestler, runaway bull, walking pile of meat. Douglas didn't have time to think of the right description as the four-hundred-pound man moved toward him at an impressive speed considering his size and with one punch sent Douglas into the air, back over his chair, and across the empty stage next to their table.

"Ah, no," Sam said, pushing himself up from his chair.

The sight of his younger brother flying through the air seemed to entertain Leo. He knocked back his shot of tequila. Watching Sam enter the fray, he yelled, "Go get 'em, Little Joe!" Leo always liked to reference the TV show *Bonanza* during a fight. And he now had a ringside seat to what promised to be one hell of a knockdown.

The drunk José was somehow on the stage just as Douglas landed on it. He picked the young kid up like a piece of wet paper and slammed him against the stripper pole. Douglas's nose was already bleeding and he heard a distinct ringing in his ears. There was a metallic taste in his mouth. He braced himself for the knockout blow that was sure to follow.

But Sam stopped the punch, one meaty hand colliding with another, and without missing a step threw an awesome right hook. It barely stunned José the runaway bull.

Angelina sighed and stared glassy-eyed at the violence happening before her, resting her chin on her hand. Just another night at the strip club. Leo thought this might be his opening. He handed her a piece of paper.

"Angelina, I wrote down my cell number. If

you ever need anything at all, don't hesitate to call."

Leo felt a gust of wind on his face and could almost sense the shadow crossing over him. He barely had a second to push back as the body of the drunk José, now airborne, landed with a crash on the table, sending it splintering at all sides. The large man finally passed out at their feet amid pieces of wood and the carpet of splinters now all around them. The bull was down for the count, but Sam didn't want to take any chances.

Sensing the mood of the room now that the restless crowd had witnessed a bit of violence, Sam thought it best to make a hasty retreat. He grabbed both brothers in his thick hands and pushed them toward the club's exit. Quickly.

Outside, the club's neon sign lit up the moonless night. They ignored the cabs waiting in front of the small club and hastily made their way across the dirt road to their Jeep.

"Oh my God," Leo said, exhilarated by the thrill of peripheral violence. "That was like a bad *Bonanza* episode."

Douglas brought up the rear, nursing his jaw. "What's a *Bonanza* episode?"

"Man, it's this great TV show about a guy with three sons all from different mothers . . . very relatable to our situation. Sammy and I used to watch the reruns when we were younger. Pretty much the only time we weren't beating each other up, right?"

"It was a stupid show," Sam replied.

The three brothers bounded into their Jeep. Sam revved the engine and pulled away from the club, eager to put some distance between them and the fight.

"No, it was a great show," Leo insisted. "Classic, iconic television. I can't believe you've never seen *Bonanza*. They didn't have Nick at Night in the slammer?"

"No," said Douglas.

"Wow," Leo continued. "You would be the perfect Little Joe. He was the youngest."

Sam smirked and turned to Leo. "Who would you be? Hoss?"

Leo shook his head. "No, no. You're Hoss. Big pecs, Popeye forearms. Perfect."

"Hoss was more defined by his stupidity than size and he was the middle child. So you'd be Hoss."

"Eat me," Leo said.

Douglas poked his head forward from the backseat. "Thanks for helping me out in there, Sam. Just like a big brother should, huh?"

Sam shook his head. "Brother? I'm a cop. I was stopping a homicide."

Leo felt a twinge of pity for the kid. "Wow—you're a dick," he said.

"It's cool, it's cool," Douglas interjected. "I don't care."

A blip of tension passed through the Jeep.

"The bottom line is," Leo said, "we have nothing on Rodriguez."

"Not necessarily," Douglas said with a grin. "She gave me her apartment number and told me to stop by. She said she was having a party."

The two brothers looked at the third as a shit-eating grin spread across his face.

Sam drove the Jeep through the main part of the city to the address Angelina had given Douglas. He pulled the Jeep next to the curb and parked. Across the street he could see the entranceway to Angelina's apartment building: clean, un-cracked cement leading to elegant glass doors and mood lighting. The Jeep, wide open all around and on top, left them nowhere to hide, no way to disguise their stakeout. Sam figured he'd have to be even more alert than usual.

He turned to the kid to give him some last-minute instructions. "Okay, don't press too hard for information. She's scared. Take it nice and easy."

Leo took one look at the goofy smile on the kid's face and had second thoughts. Third, even. "You're sending a boy in to do a man's job."

But Sam saw him coming a mile away. "She asked for the kid, Leo. Not you."

"I know," Leo countered. "But it's a party. So I can go up there and mingle . . ."

Sam stared at Leo for a beat, then cut him off with a "Yeah, whatever" and turned back to face Douglas.

"Listen, *anything* in that apartment, anything that gets us closer to Rodriguez, okay?"

Douglas nodded profusely. "I'll do my best. Wish me luck."

"Yeah, right, just go."

Sam watched the kid exit the Jeep and cross the street, walking quickly toward the stripper's apartment. He felt a tingle in his gut; something wasn't quite right. His cop instinct was telling him this was a bad idea sending the kid into a foreign environment with no weapon. No backup.

As if he could read Sam's thoughts, Leo said, "She is going to chew him up and spit him out." Because he probably didn't want to see what was going to happen next, Leo tipped his seat back and shut his eyes.

Douglas adjusted the collar of his jacket and entered the luxury apartment building, walking through the marble floors and mirrored hallways to the elevator. The metal doors closed quietly. He took the elevator up to the fourth floor.

The elevator let him out onto a serene hallway decorated with clean carpeting and pale yellow walls. Wall sconces dispersed the light.

Douglas found the apartment and knocked on the door. He could hear music through the door and wondered how he should handle the crowd of strangers no doubt waiting at the party and still look through the apartment for clues about Rodriguez. Obviously, a gringo sniffing around the place would be an easy mark. Perhaps there would be enough of a crowd to disguise his movements and help cover his tracks.

He also wondered if he'd get to see Angelina again, up close. He wouldn't mind finding clues about Rodriguez and spending some time alone with her. Maybe there would be an empty room or secluded corner where he could ask her just what her foot meant to say back at the club.

After a few seconds the door opened, producing Angelina, once again in all her glory. She was wearing a revealing black dress that ran out of material just as it crossed the top of her thighs. She flashed him a welcoming smile—all red-ruby lips and sugar-cube teeth.

"Hello," he said.

"Hello."

Her breasts were even more exposed than they'd been at the club, if that were possible, as if she'd invented a new form of gravity to keep them in the tight dress. She stared hungrily at the young kid. Douglas looked past her into the room, which was filled with nice furniture, side tables, and two lamps. But no people.

"I thought there was a party?" he asked, genuinely confused.

"There is," she said simply.

"Am I early?"

"No. You *are* the party."

With that she grabbed Douglas by the jacket and pulled him into a passionate kiss. Her lips found his and they were the softest he had ever kissed. She pulled him closer, back into the apartment. Douglas kicked the door closed behind him.

Outside on the street, Sam had slipped into surveillance mode. His gut instinct was still speaking to him, telling him to stay on high alert. He sat behind the wheel of their rented Jeep and watched the street while Leo slept, head back, mouth open. Then Sam noticed a silver Mercedes convertible, its hubcaps gleaming even in the unlit night, pull up in front of Angelina's apartment building. A man stepped gingerly out of the driver's seat. He adjusted his suit jacket and headed inside the building, passing quickly through the elegant glass doors.

Sam looked from the man to the mug shot of Edgar Rodriguez he held in his hands. It was him, no doubt about that. He looked over at Leo, still out cold. Snoring, even. Sam shook his head. Some surveillance team they made. Looked like it was up to him. Again.

• • •

Spread out on a soft bed surrounded by candles, Angelina and Douglas had just finished making love. The kid was breathing hard, having had one of the best rides of his life. Angelina's legs, he was sure, were numb.

She rolled beside him and stared at the ceiling for a moment, letting a large smile break across her face. She knew the American was special, but this . . . this she did not expect. Her body felt like liquid as she reached out for him once again.

"Thank you. Thank you, Jesus . . . for answering my prayers," she said, still breathing hard.

Douglas smiled, as if he knew exactly what her body was feeling. As if he could sense the heights he'd just brought her to. "You make too much of it. I've got a certain gift, sure, but . . ."

Before he could finish his sentence, she rolled over and kissed him passionately. She wanted to go again; she wanted the gringo to once again take her to such amazing heights.

Suddenly she heard the tiny click. The click of a gun.

Rodriguez stood in a corner of the bedroom, just off the kitchen. The gun in his right hand pointed squarely at Douglas, the keys to Angelina's apartment in his left.

Angelina whisked around to face her scorned lover. "Edgar!" she screamed.

Rodriguez's face was calm, without emotion. Emotion seemed to be the missing link in his DNA chain. His gun was raised and cocked, his voice unwavering as he spoke. "I will kill your young friend, then we will make love one last time before I kill you."

Douglas felt the bottom of his stomach fall out. He was naked and stuck in a corner, with nowhere to go. He was trapped.

"Edgar," Angelina said, obviously panicked and terrified. "You said tomorrow?"

"And because I'm early"—he motioned to Douglas—"this is okay?"

Edgar stepped closer to the bed. Douglas could tell he was about to pull the trigger.

"Edgar, please! Kill me but not him. He is an innocent and blessed by God."

The world fell away from them both, as if the only thing that still existed was the gun. It loomed large in front of them, and Douglas waited for the end to come. This was it. He had no way out.

A gunshot broke the tense silence, louder than he had expected.

Only something was different. Rodriguez stood motionless, eyes wide, staring straight ahead. His cold gun trembled slightly in front of him. A petrified Angelina and a stunned Douglas watched the would-be murderer crumple to the ground like a house of cards. It was then Douglas could see Sam standing in the hallway, his gun hot and smoking. His brother had just saved his life.

Sam walked up to the bed and looked down at Rodriguez.

"Well, there goes Leo's two hundred and fifty grand."

Douglas, relieved to still be alive, didn't miss a beat. "He's going to be disappointed."

He leaned back on the bed and stared longingly at the beautiful woman next to him, losing himself, for a moment, in her deep brown eyes. Nothing would make him happier than to go a few more rounds with her, to listen to her reach her special heights. But then he saw Sam's looming figure, and he remembered there was a dead body at the foot of the bed. So he made a quick exit. He grabbed his shoes, not even stopping to put them on.

• • •

Sam and Douglas hustled out into the warm night, toward the car. They found Leo still fast asleep, just where Sam had left him. They jumped into the open-air Jeep, and Sam fired up the engine and quickly pulled away from the curb.

They had made their escape. Douglas let out a long and grateful breath.

The speedy jerking of the car abruptly woke Leo up.

"What happened? What's going on?"

Douglas leaned up from the backseat so he was between Sam at the wheel and his confused passenger. "Rodriguez's mother lives in a small town called Vista del Fuego. Apparently he and his mother are close. He told Angelina he was going to America for a big score."

"Wait! Wait!" Leo said. "Who told you this? Was it somebody at the party?"

"Angelina. She was pretty nice."

Leo remained confused. "I don't get it. She was all buttoned up at the strip club. What made her change her mind?"

"W-well . . ." Douglas stammered. "She was . . . vulnerable." He busied himself with his shoes, tying the laces so he didn't have to make eye contact with Leo.

"What's that supposed to mean?"

Sam took it upon himself to deliver the bad news. "Leo, Rodriguez is dead."

Leo thought he was going to burst a blood vessel right there in the front seat. "What do you mean, Rodriguez is dead?"

"I mean the kid was in the sack with his girl-friend, Rodriguez showed up, so I had to shoot him."

Leo turned to Douglas, now totally confused, as if he hadn't heard the words "Rodriguez is dead." "Wait! Wait! You were sleeping with the famous stripper! How the hell . . ." Then, boom, it hit him. He suddenly realized the consequences of what Sam had said. "What did you just say? Did you say you shot Rodriguez? What about my two hundred and fifty thousand dollars?"

"We're going to go after Wills for the five-mil-lion-dollar reward," Sam said. "All we need is in-formation leading to his safe return. Rodriguez had to know where they're hiding Wills."

"Yeah! And unfortunately you shot him!"

At this, Douglas piped up. "It was pretty fortu-nate from where I was standing, though."

"Laying. You were laying, Romeo. Listen, here's his wallet. See what you can find. Anything. If we get a lead, we call the American embassy, we cash in the five million dollars, and we get on with our separate lives."

Leo hated to admit it, but with Rodriguez dead, and his bond money now down the drain, it wasn't a bad plan. In fact, he figured it was the only plan they had left.

Chapter
FOURTEEN

S am drove all night, leaving behind the lights and sounds of Mexico City as fast as the Jeep would let them. In under an hour they were on two-lane roads in the middle of nowhere, deep in the hilly Mexican desert, with nothing but blank space and a sky full of stars to light the way. Sam could not see very far beyond the scope of the Jeep's headlights, so he stuck to the road and kept their speed healthy but moderate. The lull of the open road soon found Douglas passed out in the backseat. Even Leo stopped talking, for once. Sam was grateful for the quiet.

The first hints of dawn came creeping over the desert mountains. In another hour the sun was high in the sky, already showing some of its fury.

Desert stretched out all around them on the two-lane road. They were deep in Mexico now. No turning back.

Sam stayed at the wheel, relentless if focused. Leo took on navigator duties, referring to a map in his lap, obviously confused at the meaningless squiggles of lines in front of him. Douglas was still asleep in the backseat, openmouthed, out cold.

"I have no idea where we are," Leo finally said.

But Sam didn't need the map. "We're headed northeast. This is the only road. We'll make it there eventually."

Leo folded the map and tossed it on the floor. Sam always did know where he was going. They could all count on that. Leo looked back at Douglas, bundled up against the wind of the open Jeep.

"So what do you think of the kid?" he asked.

"No way he came from the old man's loins," Sam said.

"Why is that?"

"He's not a big enough asshole."

Leo smirked. "Are you actually admitting you're an asshole?"

"We're both assholes."

Leo figured that comment was the closest he

was going to get to Sam's idea of self-reflection, but he wasn't having any of it. "No, don't drag me into your personal nightmare. I happen to be a very decent guy. Just because a drunk admits that he's a drunk doesn't make 'em any more sober."

"Just trying to bond with you, Leo," Sam said sarcastically. "I heard that misery loves company."

"Works the same way with misery or without. It just depends on the company, asshole."

The brothers rode in silence for a few moments, the wheels of the Jeep hard on the desert road beneath them.

"The kid does have a way with the ladies," Leo said. "Could be another clue as to him not being the old man's."

"Proves it's more environmental than genetic" was all Sam offered.

And the road stretched out before them.

Eventually they arrived at Vista del Fuego, a grim industrial town in the foothills leading to the higher peaks of the Sierra Madre mountains. They could see no signs in English, and Sam was already worried about their ability to communicate with the locals. They grabbed the first hotel room they could find. After forking over their money, Sam, Douglas, and Leo walked out of the run-down, transient hotel and headed toward the Jeep, now covered in dirt and mud from the ride up the mountain roads, and parked across the street, under the shade of a tree. Sam spied a bar next to the hotel called the Scorpion. There wasn't much else on the block.

"You should leave all your valuables in the trunk," he said. Sam noticed the sparse groups of locals checking them out. In ten minutes, he figured, the whole town would know about their arrival. About the new Americans and their mysterious visit.

But Leo was still griping about their accommodations. "One vacancy in this entire pissant town? C'mon, what is this, a convention destination? I've slept on bathroom floors that were bigger than that hotel room."

"I had a cell in juvy that was, like, six by six," Douglas said, trying to lighten Leo's mood. "We usually had to double up in a place like that. But if it was a slow week, I had the whole place to myself. I'm pretty lucky like that."

"Yeah, a regular horseshoe up your ass," Leo

said. "There is no way I am sleeping in a bed with either one of you guys."

Sam opened the trunk to get to their bags. "Fine," he said. "Sleep in the truck."

"C'mon," Douglas offered. "I'll take the floor. You guys take the beds."

They pulled out just what they needed, leaving the bags behind in the trunk.

"Wow, listen to him. He's a puppy dog. He's cute, cuddly, chicks dig him, and he'll sleep on the floor."

A particularly dangerous-looking man with a large scar on his cheek passed Leo on the street and gave him a threatening once-over. Sam stared hard and flexed his muscles.

"Guys, we gotta be careful," Leo said. "We stick out like sore thumbs in this town."

Douglas, oblivious to the man and his brother's apprehension, looked at the town's vista and the mountains in the backdrop. "It's beautiful here. I wish I spoke Spanish. I'd want to immerse myself in the local culture." He started to cross the road.

Leo pulled him back just as a large truck filled with army troops in black uniforms, riding with weapons in full view, passed in front of them.

"How's that for local culture?" Leo asked him. "Dive in."

Douglas followed his brothers dejectedly. After a quick stop in their small room, they headed back out to the Jeep. Soon they were back on yet another dusty two-lane road, on their way to find Rodriguez's mother.

The three brothers pulled up to a small, stucco house just outside the middle of nowhere. Bright teal paint covered the door and window frames, giving it a local flair, a bit of color amid all the dust. Plants were scattered across the front porch.

Sam knocked on the door and got no response. He knocked again and finally a woman in her fifties slowly pulled open the door. Sam could tell she was not used to finding Americans on her front step, nor did she seem very happy to see them.

"*Sí?*" she asked.

"Señora Rodriguez?" Sam asked.

She nodded.

"*Habla* English?" Sam asked her. "Do you speak any English?"

The woman shook her head. Sam wasn't surprised. This deep into Mexico, most of the locals didn't speak English.

He was about to turn away when Leo seized the moment with gusto. He stepped in front of Sam and started speaking with her in Spanish.

"Mrs. Rodriguez," Leo said with a smile, *"may we speak with your son Edgar? We are friends of his."*

Sam and Douglas exchanged surprised glances. "Hey, we've got a bilingual brother!" Douglas exclaimed. "That's going to come in handy down here."

"Yeah," Sam agreed. "Now he can get us killed in two languages."

The Mexican woman ignored the two gringos and kept her eyes on Leo. *"My son is not here. You do not look like his friends."*

"Oh, yes," Leo said. *"We go way back, Eddy and me . . . us. Do you know where we can find my good friend?"*

Señora Rodriguez eyed him warily. *"No. Are you police?"*

Leo shook his head. *"God forbid, no. We hate the police."*

Sam pulled out a picture they had taken from Rodriguez's wallet and handed it to Leo. "See if this helps." The black-and-white photo was of a beautiful young woman with bright, almond-shaped eyes and long, thick dark hair.

Leo showed the photo to Señora Rodriguez. *"Ah, yes, yes, yes. He said you would know to trust us if we showed you this."*

Señora Rodriguez looked at the picture, her wary gaze passing from it to Leo. She seemed a bit confused, as if she didn't know who to believe: the unsmiling woman in the photo or the smiling gringo on her doorstep.

Eventually, she shook her head. *"I don't even trust him."* There was a pause. Leo had hit a brick wall.

Sam tried to push her further, trying to play bad cop to Leo's good cop. "Ask about the woman in the picture. She may be in danger." But before he could say anything else, he heard a voice from behind him. Coming up on their blind side, a young boy appeared holding a very long rifle pointed right at Sam. The boy spoke to his mother in Spanish.

"Mama, can I shoot them, please?"

Señora Rodriguez crossed her arms in front of her, looking pridefully at her younger son. *"This son, I trust,"* she said.

Leo raised his arms in front of the small boy with the large gun, backing up a few steps. *"He sounds like a nice boy, Mrs. Rodriguez. We certainly mean no harm."*

Leo was intent on talking them out of this mess, but Sam was a cop, through and through. He didn't like having a gun pointed at him, even if the gun was held by a kid less than half his age. In a lightning-fast move, Sam grabbed the long barrel of the rifle and ripped it from the boy's puny hands. Sam wrapped a meaty limb around his neck and shoved the kid up against the side of the house, the plaster letting off a small cloud of dust. The boy's eyes grew wide with fear.

Señora Rodriguez's face crumpled like paper in water. She couldn't bear to see her young son hurt. He was all she had left. *"Please, no, not this one! He only protects me . . ."* Leo saw the fear in her eyes and shoved the photo back in front of her face. It was an obvious trade: the name of the girl in the photo for the safety of her son. *"Trujillo . . ."* Señora Rodriguez stammered, *"Theresa Trujillo is her name."*

"Where can we find her?" Leo asked forcefully. The kid stayed frozen against the wall, his

eyes boring into Sam, whose hand was still easily circling his throat.

Even before the woman began to give them the location of the mysterious Theresa Trujillo, Sam knew they were on to something. They finally had their first solid lead.

Chapter
FIFTEEN

Back at the compound, Wills's captors gathered in the house next to the one where they still kept the billionaire shackled and imprisoned. This house, too, was made of stone and was cool in the afternoon heat. Nealon sat calmly at a table, playing solitaire on one of Canton's many laptop computers. A cell phone with an AC power pack sat in a modem receptacle attached to the computer, the only modern fixture in the place. He was joined by Steve Bermutti, another henchman, with an expertise in home-made bombs and detonators, who was somewhat intrigued watching the explosion that was happening in front of him.

Canton paced the room like a caged animal,

gripping a local newspaper with both hands. He was obviously not happy with what he was reading. The front page, all in Spanish, was less clear than the large photo of Edgar Rodriguez, their onetime linchpin in the Kyle Wills kidnapping plan. The headline, *Known Drug Cartel Hit Man Edgar Rodriguez Found Murdered,* was easy enough to translate. Canton threw the newspaper to the ground. Bermutti leaned casually against the wall, eager to see what would happen next.

Canton was enraged, even more so in the face of Nealon's apparent calm. "Rodriguez is dead! They tracked him down here. You're gonna sit there and tell me you had this figured? Leave them little pieces of cheese to find us with? Make it more interesting?"

Nealon smirked. "An FBI agent was quoted in the article. The Bureau's claiming no responsibility."

"And you believe them?" Bermutti asked.

"I worked for them ten years. They'll consider it a huge failure if they don't bring Wills back alive. Whoever killed Rodriguez doesn't give a damn about Wills. Let me worry about it, will you?"

There was a long pause while Canton calmed

Detective Sam Carey (John Cena) awaits word of his suspension from the LAPD.

Douglas Carey (Boyd Holbrook) on the day of his release from Folsom State Prison.

Sam intervenes in a strip club brawl between Douglas and José in Mexico City.

Douglas tries to charm Theresa (Lela Loren) and her wary grandfather into giving them information about Edgar Rodriguez.

Sam and Douglas struggle to communicate with Theresa and her grandfather.

En route to track down Kyle Wills and his kidnappers, Sam rides deep into the Mexican desert.

Douglas and his white mare make a perfect team.

Sam leads his gang across the scenic but dangerous terrain.

down. Nealon's voice gave the impression of a ticking bomb—a calm and easy tone that nonetheless betrayed the growing rage just under the surface. Bermutti knew not to cross him. Nobody crossed the Iceman. He only hoped Canton knew that, too.

Nealon continued to play solitaire on the computer as if nothing had happened.

"Okay, but while you're worrying, get off my computer," Canton said. "It took me a month to put in those money transfers and you'll crash it playing cards."

"All right," Bermutti said, hoping to calm Canton down before Nealon got really angry. "Look, if the Feds didn't kill Rodriguez, then who?"

Nealon smirked again. "In the world Rodriguez lived in, I'm sure the list was endless. It doesn't matter. It's not connected."

"Yeah, except now Rodriguez is dead," Canton interjected. "We're in the middle of Mexico— and we don't have the Mexican who brought us to the dance!"

There was another long pause as Canton, catching a look from Bermutti, did his best to calm down. He breathed deeply, exhaling slowly.

"We don't need him anymore," Nealon explained. "It's all preset. But you know what, why don't we send Bertram and Bermutti into town to see if anybody's been looking around?"

And with that Bermutti pushed himself off the wall and left the room, eager to get away from Nealon, who could get violent in the presence of panic. If Canton wasn't careful, he was going to learn that lesson the hard way.

Nealon went back to his computer, content to watch the cards fall where they may. He stifled the voice inside him that wanted to get rid of Canton right now—to take him out back and put a bullet in his fat head, if only to shut him up. But they needed his computer expertise; he was the one who set up all the international accounts for the transfers from Wills's accounts. And someone had to collect the money when it came. After that, Nealon knew all bets were off.

He would make sure that, at the end of the day, he was the one holding the bag of cash.

Chapter
SIXTEEN

Señora Rodriguez's directions had been exact, and in little time Sam was driving the Jeep up to a quiet piece of land, a suburban oasis dropped down in the middle of the Mexican desert. The stucco house was freshly painted, the landscape green and well maintained. A welcoming patch of grass sat beneath a copse of trees, next to an ancient cart, its wheels rusted and sunk in the dirt.

Sam drove up the dirt path between the house and the long patch of grass. Trees dotted the area, making it seem more like a small park than the desert.

Sam parked the Jeep, now with mud speckled over its silver exterior. Sam, Leo, and Douglas exited the car and headed toward the porch.

"Hey," Sam said to Leo. "You speak Spanish. You do the talking."

"Oh. What are you saying, Sam? You saying you *need me* all of a sudden?"

"No," he replied. "It's just for some reason you seem smarter when I don't know what you're saying."

Douglas, ever the peacekeeper, stepped between them. "You think you could teach me?"

"What?" Leo asked.

"Spanish," Douglas said.

"Sure—I'll loan you the tapes."

They arrived at a polished wooden door with an ornate design and door handle. Sam knocked twice on the large door and soon, standing before them, was the woman from the photograph. In person she was even more beautiful: deep, dark eyes, flawless skin, and an intensity they could all immediately sense. Her strength was evident even from this initial glimpse of her.

Theresa looked them over and then spoke in perfect English. "Can I help you?"

"Really?" Leo said, disappointed. "You speak English?" His chance to be the leader was now gone. But before Leo could finish, Sam took the lead.

"Theresa. We're friends of Edgar Rodriguez. He told us . . ."

She cut him off cold.

"He's dead. Did you know that about your friend Edgar?" She crossed her arms. It was apparent she didn't believe a word they said. "Are you police?"

"Geez, everybody's just paranoid about cops around here, aren't they?" Leo said, staring at Sam. "I guess it crosses all borders, right?"

But Sam was getting impatient. She was their one solid lead and he wasn't going to lose it. They needed answers and they needed them fast. "We're not police. Did you happen to hear anything about the kidnapping of the American?"

"I can read," she said sarcastically. "If you're not police, you should leave or my grandfather's going to blow a large hole through this door and ruin it."

At that, Sam took out his old police ID and held it up for her to see.

"Well, in that case, I lied. Just heard Mexicans were friendly people."

Theresa eyed the badge warily. "I'm half Indian. We're not so friendly."

Theresa moved aside to give the three brothers room to enter her home. As she opened the door, they saw her grandfather standing there with a very angry look on his face and a very large, double-barrel shotgun in his hands. He remained standing close by Theresa as she motioned them inside. Leo and Douglas looked around the room while Sam remained vigilant, keeping one eye on the grandfather's shotgun.

Theresa, obviously annoyed at the intrusion of the three gringos, remained cold and clipped. "I have not seen Edgar in two years."

"Your picture was in his wallet," Sam said, leading the interrogation.

Theresa remained unaffected. Composed. "I can assure you there is no picture of him in my wallet. You can check."

Sam wanted to, very badly. He sensed there was something she wasn't telling them. But then Douglas interrupted.

"There's no need," he said to Theresa. Both brothers gave him a strange look. "She's telling the truth, Sam."

Sam just stared back at Douglas like he was insane. *Who is this kid?* he wondered yet again.

"What, now you got a crystal ball up your

ass?" asked Leo. "How's that fit with the lucky horseshoe?"

"I just know. But I can only do it with women."

Sam felt like he was about to go off on the kid for interrupting his questioning. But Theresa, of course, seemed charmed and intrigued by Douglas.

"You're not a cop, are you?" she said to the young kid.

"No." He motioned to Sam. "I'm his brother." He then nodded toward Leo. "His, too."

"She doesn't need to know all that," Leo said quickly.

Sam tried to focus the interview again. "How do you know Rodriguez?"

"We grew up together" was all she said.

Douglas tried a different tack. "We don't know anything about your beautiful country. We could really use some help right now." He shot her his best puppy-dog look.

Theresa stayed silent.

"There's a reward for information leading to the return of the rich American," Sam said. "We'll pay an equal share."

"An equal share—are you crazy?" Leo yelled. "Ten percent, max."

Before Sam could respond, Theresa answered them both. "I want no part of it. When I found out Edgar died, I felt nothing."

Sam studied her for one more beat. Her features were even. No quick ticks, no body language to give her away. Sam had interrogated hundreds of criminals during his career. There was always something that gave them away. But not so with her.

"If she is lying, she's damn good," Sam concluded.

"She's not," Douglas insisted.

Theresa was tired of their worthless banter. She wanted the three strangers out of her house. "It's time for you to leave."

Her grandfather raised the shotgun and leveled it at the brothers once again. They had nothing to do but concede. Leo and Douglas headed for the door, following Sam.

"Back to square one," Leo said under his breath. He tipped his hat to Theresa as he walked out the door. "Charmed," he said, his voice dripping with sarcasm.

Douglas was the last to leave and Theresa looked gently at him as he passed her. She touched him softly on the arm.

"Sorry, we're just kind of outta place here and . . ."

"Thank you. You are very kind," she offered.

"We appreciate your help."

Douglas left her with a smile.

The three brothers walked back toward the Jeep. Sam was angry that his questioning of Theresa went nowhere—and how could it? His two brothers kept interrupting him every step of the way. Sam remembered now why most cops preferred to work alone. He was no exception.

"I thought they would've taken your badge when they fired your ass," Leo said, catching up to him.

"I wasn't fired, I was suspended. I keep an old badge, just in case." As if it mattered. Sam was suspended, their investigation into Wills's kidnapping was going nowhere, and Sam was damn tired of playing babysitter to these two amateurs.

"Kid," he said, turning on Douglas. "Rule number one in team play. Never tell anybody anything until we talk."

"If we talked about it, would you have asked for her help?"

"No!"

"Oh," Leo said, jumping in, "but it's completely okay for you to offer a complete stranger an equal share, huh? What the hell is that? You know, there's no *I* in *team*, Sammy boy."

"But there is in *family*, and I'm still the oldest. So shut up!"

The two brothers recoiled at the volume of Sam's voice. But he was fed up, completely and totally. Their trail was at a dead end. Their one lead wasn't talking. Wills was still being held in some unknown location by a group of unknown assailants, kidnapped in broad daylight on the streets of Los Angeles. They were up the creek without a paddle. And if they didn't think of something soon, this entire trip would have all been for nothing.

Chapter
SEVENTEEN

No one spoke during the ride back to the hotel. Frustration had settled over them all like the desert dust covering the Jeep. Sam pulled up across from the hotel and once again noticed the bar down the street. The clapboard sign over the entrance was covered in grime and dirt, the red painted letters of *The Scorpion* barely visible in the afternoon glare. Sam was already regretting the decision, but he didn't think they had a lot of options.

"You want to know what's going on in a neighborhood, you go to a local bar."

Leo eyed the place warily. "This is the local bar you go to if you want to get shot for no apparent reason."

"You speak the language, Leo," Douglas added. "They'll respect that."

Sam almost laughed. "You bet. How do I beg for my life in Spanish? Just so I know."

Just then Leo reached into his jacket and pulled out a .357 Magnum. "This is how you beg for your life in Spanish."

Sam and Douglas both gaped at the sheer size of the gun. It almost dwarfed his hand.

"Good God, Leo. You hunting bear?" Douglas said from the backseat.

"You got a license for that?" Sam asked.

"I'm a bail bondsman, not a kindergarten teacher. You packing that baby-cop little pea-shooter of yours?"

"It'll do." Sam turned to the backseat. "Got anything you can use, kid?"

"I don't care for guns," Douglas said. He always figured a good thief should never have the need for one.

"Okay, you'll make a fine-looking corpse. Just wait here and keep the engine running."

Sam and Leo exited the Jeep and walked toward the bar. Douglas jumped into the front seat and watched them go. "Be careful!" he said, almost to himself.

• • •

The bar's interior looked trapped in dust. It was everywhere—on the empty wooden tables, the pool table in back, the windows that still let in a generous amount of light. Groups of twos and threes were huddled over various bottles of tequila, and they, too, looked trapped, protecting their tables and the bottles and staring at the two brothers as they walked into the place.

Sam and Leo took a seat at the long bar, the two stools offering what Sam felt was the fastest and easiest getaway back out the door. Mariachi music played in the background, interrupted by the loud *thwack* of the pool balls as a game began.

A shot of tequila slid along the bar top and came to rest in Leo's hand. Sam got one, too, and both of them downed the shots. The tequila burned going down. Leo handled the foul-tasting rotgut well, but it took Sam a second to adjust to the burning down his throat. Leo noticed and enjoyed the moment. The bartender did, too.

"What's the matter?" he asked Sam in Spanish. *"Choke on the worm?"*

Leo tried to butter up the bartender. *"No, he's just not used to the fine quality. A real pussy."*

The bartender chuckled and walked away.

"What was that about?" Sam asked. He was uneasy in the dirty place and not knowing the language was making things worse for him.

"You see what me speaking the language does? It turns the tables and puts me in control. And I can see how much you hate it."

"You know, Leo, this isn't a competition. You could get your head blown off in a place like this."

"Fair enough. But I do enjoy watching you squirm, Sam."

Sam continued to eye the crowd. The alcohol and grime couldn't cover one very clear fact: everyone in the joint was watching them. Closely. This was not a place that welcomed strangers.

"You're right, no one makes a move around here without the cartels finding out about it."

"I figure everybody in this town is employed by them, one way or another."

"Right. Act like we're here doing business. See if we can buy some information."

Leo was a bit surprised at Sam's suggestion. "So basically you want me to pretend we want to buy drugs?"

"When in Rome, Leo. See if you can get something from the bartender."

Leo looked at his brother for a beat, then figured what the hell. The bartender seemed pretty friendly, not too dirty, and as he was wearing only a small T-shirt, Leo was fairly certain he wasn't carrying a gun. He motioned the bartender over to them.

"Two more tequilas, my friend," Leo said to him in Spanish. *"Go easy on my partner here."* The bartender poured two more shots and set them down. Leo reached for the drink and leaned in close, lowering his voice. *"So . . . who would a couple of businessmen talk to if they were looking to . . . do some business around here?"*

The bartender remained friendly. Leo took it as a good sign. *"Depends on the business."*

"Well, if I wanted to buy the best shoes, I'd be in Italy, wouldn't I?"

The bartender nodded. *"Nobody buys anything around here without talking to Verdugo."*

Leo stared at his brother, who was getting increasingly edgy not knowing what was going on, and he could barely hide his satisfaction.

"Okay. And where can I find Verdugo?"

The bartender's demeanor changed instantly.

His face turned to stone and the smile disappeared. *"You don't. Verdugo finds you."* He took a few steps back from the bar.

Sam watched the exchange feeling an increasing level of panic. His antennae were up instantly. Something was wrong. They had to get out of there now.

Right on cue the front doors of the cantina flew open in a burst of noise and dust. Several Mexican policemen surged through the door. The locals jumped up from their tables, upending them and sending bottles to the floor. The policemen pulled something into the bar after them. It was Douglas. Handcuffed with a gun to his temple.

"Ah, crap," said Leo.

The lead policeman spoke English, but his tone would have been apparent in any language. "Gentlemen. Your friend here was double parked. Put your weapons on the bar."

Sam knew they were screwed. No way out. Ambushed by these fake policemen. He scowled as he placed his gun on the bar while Leo did the same, giving up their only method of defense. Sam could only guess what would happen to them next.

●　　●　　●

The elegant mansion was isolated on a small bluff, a haven in the middle of the Mexican desert. The purple shading on the mountains meant the long day was coming to a close, the sun losing most of its strength to the coming dusk. The mansion looked like a small fortress amid the brush and vegetation of the desert, nestled between opposing mountains with only one road leading up to it. No doubt the guards could see for miles, which eliminated the chance of unwanted visitors.

The two Humvees drove quickly up the entry road and through heavily fortified gates manned with security personnel. Sam thought of Iraq and Afghanistan, other war zones he'd seen on the news, and shuddered that this fortress, armed to the teeth with automatic guns and half an army, was located not half a world away in the Middle East but just a short flight from Los Angeles. It seemed like another world unto itself.

The three brothers were pushed out of the Humvees and moved at gunpoint to the far side of the fortress. There, too, another world emerged. The wide vista gave way to a manicured lawn, a beautiful pool with a natural stone waterfall, and a killer desert view. They could have been in the backyard of a suburban mansion instead of being captured and taken to face the local head of the powerful drug cartel.

Tito Verdugo was in his midfifties, Sam guessed, and looked pleasant enough in the backyard surroundings. He leisurely read the newspaper on wicker patio furniture, a drink set on the table before him. He looked more like someone's grandfather than the most violent drug lord of the region. But Sam the cop knew that things were rarely what they seemed to be.

The three brothers, bound and gagged, were brought before Verdugo. The man barely looked up from the newspaper as one of the henchmen removed the gag from Sam's mouth. His throat felt dry from the dust and the heat.

Finally, Verdugo looked up at Sam and met his stare. Verdugo's eyes were cold and dead: the eyes of a killer. He waited for Sam to speak.

"We think the American, Wills, may be hidden down here."

"And you assume I have something to do with it?" Verdugo asked, amused.

"No. You have no motive."

"Good. At least you're not a stupid police-man. What, then?"

"If Edgar Rodriguez brought him down here, I assume he asked your permission. Out of respect. Or at least good sense."

Verdugo dismissed the comment with a wave of his manicured hand. "Rodriguez had no respect and little sense. He worked for me. He wanted to be me. Can you blame him?" Verdugo motioned to his mansion estate, the green, well-kept lawns around him, the crystal-clear blue swimming pool with a waterfall that mimicked the rock formations all around them.

"Could the kidnappers be down here without you knowing about it?" Sam asked.

"If they are here, it is because Rodriguez knew where to hide them. In a place where I would have no concern."

"Does that place exist? Is there a place where people aren't afraid of you?"

Verdugo smiled. "To know me is to be afraid. And if they are within a thousand miles in any direction, they know me."

"What kind of place would not concern you?"

"Simple. A place where the soil is not fertile. I am a farmer, remember."

"What about the Indian land?" Sam asked.

"Doubtful. They have their holy places, but there the Indians would have killed them by now. Maybe the canyons."

"If Wills is here, the U.S. government is going to bring more heat on you than you can afford. I want to find him first. I need your help."

There was a long pause. Sam hoped Verdugo would see the logic in his argument—that while Verdugo had no care whether they lived or died, they might at least prove useful enough to him not to be killed on the spot.

Verdugo cleared his throat. The icy stare was back, the dead look of a cold and hardened killer. "Even if I did have something to do with it, your government couldn't prove it. You will be dropped off back at your hotel. If you are not gone in twenty-four hours, you will die here."

Verdugo turned back to his newspaper and made a slight gesture with his hand, as if he were merely swatting a fly. His henchmen grabbed Sam and his brothers and led them away.

The three brothers were pushed back toward the Humvees. A million scenarios were running through Sam's head, things he remembered about Mexican cartels from his work on the force. He made eye contact with Leo, still bound and gagged, and caught something new in his eyes: fear. Every plan Sam came up with in his head ended in the same way: with one or both of his brothers getting killed.

Chapter
EIGHTEEN

Bermutti, the explosives expert, had kept an eye on the hotel for most of the afternoon. He had heard about the three gringos arriving in town, one looking suspiciously like an American cop. He figured it was a good thing Nealon had sent him and Bertram into town to snoop around. Something was definitely up—and Rodriguez's murder was just the beginning of it. He had sent Bertram out on another errand while he grabbed his supplies and bribed the hotel clerk into letting him have a look around the Americans' room. He was in and out in less than five minutes, and now he was waiting patiently in his car across the street from the hotel. Waiting to see the room's light turn on and for the fireworks to begin.

Piece of cake, he thought.

He wondered what Bertram was doing to the woman, the bitch.

It wasn't hard to sneak into the unguarded house, the one with the ornate wooden door and flimsy lock. Bertram moved soundlessly into the front room and found the woman alone. She fought back bravely at first, almost as if she didn't believe he would actually hit a woman. Bertram of course had no such qualms. He had been hit or slapped for most of his life and so it felt good to give back to the world everything that had been given to him, so bountifully, since he was a young boy.

He grabbed her long, thick hair and punched her twice, drawing blood quickly. It was a shame to bloody such a beautiful face, but still, a job was a job. She glared furiously at him, even with her own blood on her face and his gun by her cheek. Bertram almost respected that. It was clear to him that the fun was just beginning.

"Who were they?" he asked her, moving the metal gun against her cheek.

Theresa winced in pain. "I don't know, you pig!"

"You're gonna tell me, and you're gonna tell me right now!" he yelled.

The slightest noise, a small click, reached Bertram's ears. Having grown up around guns and worked with them most of his life, he was trained to notice such a sound. In one fluid motion, he swung his body around and took aim, noticing the old man with the double-barrel shotgun poised in the hallway. He fired one shot right into the old man's heart. A red bloom sprouted over his white shirt.

Theresa looked over and saw her grandfather's lifeless body slumped on the floor. A pool of red was spread out underneath him.

"No, Papa, no . . ." she yelled. His body was the last thing she saw before her world, too, went black.

Chapter
NINETEEN

The sleek black truck pulled up in front of the Hotel del Fuego, sending the cockroaches on the ground scurrying for cover across the empty, dirty street. Sam, Leo, and Douglas were unceremoniously lifted from the flatbed of the truck and tossed out onto the street by Verdugo's lackeys. The truck raced away as they got up and dusted themselves off. Sam was getting very tired of being pushed around.

Each of them was a bit rattled from their visit to Verdugo, not to mention his threat to kill them if they didn't leave town. They had twenty-four hours. No plan, no lead on Wills's whereabouts, and now no guns. It was that lack of planning, Sam knew, that could very likely get them all killed. Shot in the head and dropped in a ditch. No one in town would even blink.

"What do we do now?" Leo asked.

"We get the hell out of here," Sam said.

"Are you kidding me? What about my money?"

"I go back to work in three weeks. This," Sam said, motioning to the deserted street, the headlights of the truck that had just tossed them out on their asses still visible on the horizon, "is ridiculous."

Sam headed for the hotel, eager to put this mess behind him. He didn't see any other way to handle this. Verdugo would kill them—Sam had no doubt about that. He had to protect his brothers, and that meant getting out of town as quickly as they could.

But Leo was panicked. He ran in front of Sam and blocked his way. "You really gonna walk away from this whole thing, three million dollars for each of us? I don't get my piece without you."

Sam said, "It ain't worth getting killed over."

A pained look crossed Leo's face. "It is for me."

"Give it up, Leo," Sam said, not wanting to acknowledge the look of desperation on his brother's face. He pushed Leo aside and headed into the hotel. Leo stood alone in the street, destroyed.

"I've got nothing left!" he yelled to Sam's back.

Sam entered the lobby and didn't look back. He couldn't. Leo's words filled his head and made it hurt to think. This couldn't be Leo's only chance—could he really have fallen that far? Had his life failed so completely that he had no other recourse than to risk it all by going against a Mexican drug lord for the sake of money?

Sam barely noticed Douglas at his heels. The kid followed him into the hotel lobby.

"Sam, at least think about it on the way home. Finally meeting my family has meant a lot to me and . . ."

Sam spun around and got in Douglas's face.

"We ain't family. If there's no money involved in this, we never meet! What does that tell you?"

Sam continued on his way. But Douglas wasn't giving up just yet.

"I don't care about the money. I'm just glad to meet you guys. I just wish I could've met my dad, too."

Sam stopped. He'd reached his limit. It was bad enough seeing his brother brought to his knees, risking his life for some stupid reward money, but he'd be damned if he was going to let this young kid airbrush the past.

"Okay, let's bring you up to speed on your family. Your 'dad' was an abusive drunk and a sex addict. Four kids, four mothers!"

"All right," Douglas said, trying to absorb the information while ignoring the rage and fury all over Sam's face. "Did you at least get the chance to meet your mom?"

"Yeah. Stripper. Raised me for three years, put me on a doorstep, see ya, bye."

Douglas's face started to fall. This wasn't what he'd expected at all. "What about Leo's mother?"

"A cleaning woman for dad's bookie. Died in childbirth. Oh, don't worry. He and Nina's mother had a pretty good run. Three or four years. They were drunk the whole time."

Sam almost couldn't stop himself. Just revisiting the past made him angrier than he'd been in years—even more so than the day he pummeled that perp on the steps of the courthouse, the act that led to his suspension. He couldn't escape the past when his brothers were around; they were constant walking reminders of everything he'd tried to leave behind. And that's why they had to leave town. Be done with Mexico and go their separate ways. If not, Sam felt he was going to lose his mind. Or start pummeling again.

Sam made his way up the stairs to the second floor of the hotel and headed down the hallway to their room, with Douglas following at his heels.

"He must have had some good qualities, right?" Douglas said hopefully. It was clear that whatever fantasies he held about his father and this new family he had found were fading away quickly.

"Oh, he sure did," Sam replied. "He'd only beat up Leo because he wouldn't hit a girl and he was afraid of me." Sam turned to open the door to their room, but Douglas stopped him.

Douglas peered at the doorframe of their room and pulled Sam back. He dropped his voice to a whisper. "I rigged the door. Kids were always sneaking into rooms in juvy." He pulled out a paper clip that he had lodged in the molding over the door. It was bent out at a ninety-degree angle. Someone obviously had opened the door and bent the wire back.

That was it for Sam. He let the rage flow freely, and it enveloped him.

He made a beeline for the stairwell and took

the stairs two at a time back down to the lobby. It was deserted except for the desk clerk. Sam had him in his sights. He grabbed the man and slammed him up against the wall. Plaster dust jettisoned into the air. The clerk practically trembled with fear as Sam's huge forearm was placed against his windpipe. The clerk was small and thin, couldn't weigh much over 140 pounds. Sam could snap him into pieces with one hand tied behind his back.

"Could be somebody's still there, could be somebody wired the room. Either way, you gave him a key and told him the room, because it wasn't broken into." Sam's words all came out in a rush. He could barely contain his anger enough to form sentences.

The clerk's look of fear soon gave way to one of guilt. Eager to breathe again, he didn't even try to cover up his crime. "Please, a man was here looking for you but he's gone."

"One of Verdugo's men?"

"No. American. I did not know him."

Great, Sam thought. Now someone else—someone new—was out to get them.

He pulled the clerk off the wall and forced him up the stairs, back to the hallway outside their room. He waved Leo and Douglas off, and they kept a safe distance at the top of the stairs. Sam led the clerk to their room.

"Open it," Sam said.

The clerk was sweating bullets. He opened the door slowly, waiting for God knows what. But nothing happened. The clerk looked back at Sam and smiled.

"You see? Nothing."

The clerk reached inside the room for the light switch.

"WAIT!" Sam yelled.

Sam barely had time to jump away from the door before the heat and force of the explosion blew it back out into the hallway in a shower of splinters and fire. He felt it before he heard it— the tremendous heat and gust of air that threw him halfway down the hallway. Windows shattered as the explosion rocked the rest of the hotel.

Sam found himself on top of the dumbfounded clerk about fifteen feet from the charred entrance to his room. Leo and Douglas were similarly thrown farther down the hallway and were just as shaken by the blast. Leo wiped the dust from his jacket and said to the clerk, "This your idea of 'express checkout,' asshole?"

The three brothers, their ears still ringing from the explosion, walked out in front of the hotel. Sam now knew that Americans were behind the planting of the bomb in their room, just as Americans were behind Wills's kidnapping. So was the bomb some kind of retribution for killing Rodriguez? Or was it a warning, or something else entirely? Sam couldn't answer any of the questions racing through his mind. But somehow this crazy mess was starting to make a little bit of sense.

"Same guys who kidnapped Wills. They know Rodriguez is dead. They made the connection somehow."

"How'd they know it was us?" Douglas asked.

"Because we're the only morons with bull's-eyes on our foreheads," Leo conceded.

The three brothers walked toward the Jeep. Debris and smoking wood from the hotel explosion littered the street. Then, from out of the deep, dark night, a single voice reached their ears.

"You still need help?"

The boys turned to face Theresa. She cut an imposing figure in the shadow of the hotel, half cast in its darkness. She wore a sleek leather jacket, her long hair pulled back from her face in a ponytail. She carried a rucksack slung over one shoulder. Her face was still beautiful but bruised and somehow hardened, her eyes set even deeper in her face. Even in the dim light of the hotel they could sense that something was different. Something was terribly wrong.

"What are you doing here?" Sam asked, almost afraid of the answer.

Her voice was cold and calm, betraying no emotion. "These men that worked with Edgar. Americans. They came looking for you. They killed my grandfather."

All three brothers hated to hear the words. Douglas let out a "My God." Sam berated himself. He should have seen this coming. Leo was right. They did stick out in this town. Everything they did, every act, was traceable right back to them. They should have been more careful. And now the old man had paid the price for their negligence.

"I know every road, trail, and canyon for a hundred miles," Theresa continued. She was offering her help, without saying so directly. She wanted vengeance. She locked eyes with Sam, and he could feel it pouring out of her.

She was strong, but beyond that Sam could see the cracks. She was in shock, grieving, and that made her unstable. She could get them all killed.

He shook his head, just slightly, more of a reflex than a response. But she caught it, sensing his hesitation immediately.

She started to walk away.

But Sam surprised himself. Every cop instinct in him told him to let her go. But this was the second time today they were almost killed. Two events that easily could have been avoided if they had been more aware of their surroundings and more careful in their actions in an unknown town. They were on foreign ground. They didn't know the landscape. And he was fresh out of ideas. He needed help. And she was the only one volunteering for the job.

Sam's voice was resigned, almost tender. "We're gonna need guns."

Chapter
TWENTY

The night turned darker, the sky black, as they traveled the gravel road over the short hills surrounding the small town. The now battered Jeep pulled up alongside a copse of shrubs moving slowly in the wind. Theresa served as their guide, just like she said she would, navigating Sam through the thin lanes and hills of the desert. Her knowledge of the area was indeed extensive; to Sam it appeared that she had an almost uncanny ability to guide them through the terrain, even in the dead of night.

"Stop here. We're close."

Led by Theresa, the boys exited the car and climbed up the hill, past the trees. They peered down at a small armory building. It was smaller than an airplane hangar, sheet metal covering the sides and the roof. A few armed guards patrolled the site, one on each side of the small metal building. Sam focused on the smaller guard, the one with a long rifle who was leaning casually against a dusty Jeep.

"It used to be a weapons depot for the military," Theresa explained. "Now Verdugo uses it."

Great. Now they were stealing from the head of the cartels. Sam figured it didn't matter. "What the hell. He was going to kill us anyway."

"How are we going to get in there?" Leo asked. "They gotta have some fancy alarm or locks or something, no?"

"Don't worry about it," Douglas said with confidence. "You guys take care of the guards, and I'll get you in."

On the edge of the forest surrounding the armory, Theresa waited alone as the guard walked toward her side of the building. She removed her jacket, leaving only the thin white blouse to protect her from the chilly night. She let her hair down and unbuttoned her blouse, revealing an ample distraction. Then she stepped out and made her way toward the guard. She called out to him in Spanish.

"Excuse me, sir. I ran my car into a ditch on the road above and need your help."

The guard took one look at her, a beautiful woman appearing out of nowhere in the night, and his eyes grew wide at this piece of good luck that had fallen into his lap.

"Anything I can do would be my pleasure," he said.

The guard was so distracted by Theresa's flawless beauty that he didn't even notice Sam sneak up behind him, using the shadows to hide.

Sam said, "Señor?"

The guard spun around quickly, only to meet Sam's crushing right cross. It felled him with one blow, and he crumpled uselessly to the ground, unconscious.

Theresa looked at the guard lying on the ground and then made her way to the other side of the building. She walked more confidently now, swaying her hips and keeping her head high. Her white blouse glowed in the moonlight.

The second guard, sitting on a barrel, noticed her instantly. At first he thought she was a vision or mirage, so unexpected, and so incredibly beautiful. He called out to her in Spanish.

"Hey, what the hell are you doing out—?" But

before he could finish his sentence, Leo moved up behind him and stuck a large stick into his back, mimicking a gun. The guard instantly raised his hands.

"Hand her your gun, friend," Leo said in Spanish. The guard gave Theresa his gun. She pointed it at him confidently, a triumphant smile spreading across her face.

Douglas got to work, pulling his pick kit from his jacket pocket and spreading it out on the dirt. Both guards were bound and gagged a few feet away, immobile and defeated. Douglas's hands worked quickly, deftly, his mind focused on trying to solve the puzzle of the lock. That's what he'd been taught: that every lock, no matter how heavy or thick, was just that. Just a puzzle, waiting to be solved.

Leo hovered closely behind him. "Why don't we just shoot the lock? It's gonna be a lot faster if I just shoot it."

"Great," Sam said, "so if the gunshot doesn't bring the whole town, your big mouth will. Shut up."

Douglas tried to ignore their quarreling, their bickering, their breath on his neck. "You guys mind giving me a little room?"

"Sure," Leo said. But neither he nor Sam moved.

"Where'd you learn this stuff?" Sam asked him.

"I met a guy when I was a kid. We called him Uncle Jimmy. Best B-and-E man in the country. He taught me how to get in and out of anything."

"So . . ." Leo said. "Where'd Uncle Fagin end up? San Quentin?"

"If he did, he probably broke out by now."

And with that, Douglas was finished. The puzzle was solved. He pulled the heavy lock open and dropped it on the ground.

They opened the door slowly, the guns they had taken from the guards raised and leading the way. Leo flipped on a light switch near the door, and the small room was illuminated by an overhead fluorescent light. Inside, it was a veritable candy store for the Michigan Militia and NRA enthusiasts. Automatic weapons, dynamite, hand grenades, rocket launchers, mortar shells, and many other kinds of ammunition filled the room, displayed neatly on shelves and against the walls. It looked like the armory for a small army, a very well-funded, totally outfitted army.

"This must be what Charlton Heston's first wet dream looked like," Leo said. He walked over to a wall and pulled an AK-47 down from a rack. "This'll do."

Douglas looked uneasily around the room. His elation had faded quickly. "You'll have to show me how to use one of these," he said.

Leo was nonplussed. "You know, kid, I have absolutely no idea. But I'm sure big, bad Sammy the cop knows all about it."

Sam grabbed the assault rifle and looked it over. "No. Only the bad guys get these." He hadn't seen this much weaponry, outside of the evidence locker, in years. Verdugo was armed to the teeth, and that made him even more dangerous. They were definitely treading on thin ice. One wrong move could get them killed. Twice. First by the Americans who were holding Wills, and now by Verdugo, who had already threatened their lives—and this was before they had decided to break into his armory and steal his guns.

"Just grab a good high-powered automatic rifle and some of those grenades," Sam said. "And, Leo, don't blow yourself up."

Chapter
TWENTY-ONE

Wills remained alone in the room. The laptop was cold and black, powered off, in front of him. It was, he realized, his only tether to the real world. How could a man who'd amassed so much be left with so little? He stumbled over how he got here, what kind of man he'd become, and slowly pushed down the conscience trying to rise up through his stomach like bile. He figured this was part of their tactic: to let him stew alone in his thoughts, make him become desperate, compliant, and conciliatory. It was working.

Canton slowly peeked his head into the empty room. "How do you feel, boss?"

Wills struggled with how to answer the question. Only one word came to mind. "Sorry."

Canton smiled. "Well, listen to you. I do believe that apology is sincere. Nothing like a peek at mortality to sharpen hindsight."

Canton's low, even voice sounded almost friendly. In a strange way, Wills was glad for the company. He had spent most of his time here alone and isolated, with nothing to distract him from his thoughts. His ankles hurt where they were chained to the floor. His feet were often numb. His back ached from slumping over on the cot, his hands trapped and bound.

"My life's been about money. I have trouble seeing past it."

Canton reacted in mock surprise. "Don't tell me. And now you're wondering if the money is what life is about, right?"

Wills looked up at Canton, not at all sure where this was going. The friendly tone in his voice was gone, replaced by something sinister.

"That's clichéd, man, but I'm with you," Canton said. "Because that is the question. Is the money enough?" Canton paused for effect, hoping to let the quiet, still room work over Wills's nerves.

Suddenly Canton produced a gun from behind his back and aimed it directly at Wills's head. The captive was so surprised he could barely draw a breath.

"I mean, is anything less than blowing your head off enough? Because that's the thing about blowing someone's head off. Oh, boy, it is definitely enough."

The gun hung in midair as if it had a mind of its own. Its compact barrel like an evil eye focused right on Wills. As if it could see right into him, right down to his core.

Wills braced for the impact. At close range, he probably wouldn't feel a thing. Or he would feel everything. He summoned up the courage for a few final words. They came out in a whisper. "If you're going to kill me, could I say good-bye to my family first?"

Canton appeared almost sympathetic. He moved the gun slightly away from Wills's head. "What—tell them you love them, that sort of nonsense?"

"Yes. Please."

"Wow. That is touching."

With that, Canton put the gun to Wills's head and pulled the trigger. Several times. *Click, click, click, click.* Each time, Wills jumped slightly, eyes closed, every muscle in his body tense. He waited to feel the pain, feel the bullets piercing his skin. He waited for his life to flash before his eyes, for the regret to settle in, the lingering pain of not being able to say good-bye to his wife or his son.

Of course, the gun wasn't loaded.

"Relax, will you? I can't even figure out how to load it. Not really a gun kind of guy." Canton started laughing as Wills slowly realized that he was still alive.

Canton's laugh followed him out the door, its malice lingering in the now empty room. Wills slumped over on the cot, his bound hands dragging against the cold stone floor. He was alive. Not bleeding. No bullet punctured his skin. Yet Wills couldn't help but feel completely broken.

Something about having a gun pointed at his head worked over the billionaire. Everything that had happened to him—the kidnapping, the murder of his driver and bodyguards, and now his own life so easily threatened by others—it all washed over him like a strong wave. Something in his own actions had triggered this dangerous series of events. He had done bad things, very bad things—to these men, perhaps, and to many others. And he had been brought here to the middle of nowhere to answer for those actions. The biggest surprise, at least to Wills, was that he could think of no amount of money that could rectify that. For the first time in his professional life, he had no defense against these men's accusations.

Chapter
TWENTY-TWO

Daybreak. A plain, unmarked road, once again leading them through the middle of nowhere. Large, nondescript mountains marked the horizon, which was often lost to the blaring sun. What lay ahead of them looked exactly like what lay behind them, and to Sam there was something disconcerting about this mirrored view, as if their direction did not matter at all. Backwards, forwards, sideways—each one looked the same. There was nowhere to hide in such a flat and wide mesa.

But Sam drove the Jeep faster and farther. Theresa sat beside him. Her sense of location so far had been uncanny, as if she truly knew every inch of the desert terrain. All through the night she led their way, navigating the back roads and wild paths that had brought them to this place.

Douglas and Leo were camped out in the back. Ample supplies of guns and ammunition were stored in the trunk behind them, lifted from Verdugo's armory the night before.

When they came upon the crest of a hill, Theresa signaled for Sam to slow down. "Only one road takes us close to the canyons, and they will see us coming for miles. We'll need horses."

Leo recoiled at this idea. "No, no way. I don't do horses."

Theresa looked over at Sam. He trusted her instincts now, and he could see how visible they would be traversing across such open terrain.

"You any good with a horse, kid?" Sam asked Douglas.

"Yeah. I spent a few years on a work ranch for delinquents."

"Heigh-ho, Silver!" Leo said dejectedly. He was outnumbered. He had no doubt that soon he would be on a horse.

"The Mennonites have the best horses," Theresa explained. "Supplies also."

"Mennonites?" Sam asked.

"My ass hurts already," Leo added.

• • •

They soon arrived at a rustic patch of land set behind a thicket of trees, bordered by a homemade wooden fence. A black horse-drawn carriage clip-clopped alongside the ranch, heading out toward the main road. Sam could see a handful of Mennonites working out in the fields and repairing a downed section of fence. He could see white-frame and adobe buildings, everything in its rightful place. And not an automobile in sight. It was like they had stepped back in time.

Sam pulled the Jeep close to the stables, and they were welcomed by a Mennonite in his forties who introduced himself as Karl with a slight German accent. He led them up to an adobe structure with a wooden gate. Horses leaned out over the gate, as if sensing they had guests. In the distance, a corral let a few of the horses wander around in the afternoon heat, keeping mostly to themselves. A white mare, beautiful but obviously skittish, wandered by the fence.

Leo did not waste any time explaining his needs to Karl. "Sir, I'm going to need a really gentle one. I'd like to smell the glue."

The Mennonite smiled. Theresa spied a beautiful brown horse, tall and strong, a white patch spreading across the front of its face. Its eyes were deep and noble. "The roan is beautiful," she said, running her hand gently across the side of its face.

"An excellent choice," Karl said. "You know horses."

But Leo was not distracted. "You got one where my feet could still touch the ground?"

Douglas pulled away from the others, drawn to the white mare standing alone in the corral. He approached her slowly. She was beautiful, bright white and graceful, but Douglas noticed something in the horse's eyes. She looked about with great fluctuations, as if in fear. He instinctively sensed that something was not right. The horse was ill at ease, and she bristled at his gentle touch. Suddenly, she squared off with him. He kept his eyes steady on hers and approached her carefully. Karl stood behind him and off to the side. He had learned the hard way not to get too close to this particular horse.

"She won't take a saddle," Karl said.

Douglas moved slowly to the side of the horse and began to run his hands along the horse's back and side, along her belly, and across her hocks. The horse reacted in fits and starts to his touch, as if she was sensitive in certain areas, and moved away from Douglas, gun-shy. Finally, he turned to Karl.

"She's been abused."

Karl grew defensive. "Abuse? No. Some require a firm hand."

Douglas exhaled in disgust. "Yeah, she's been burned by the hobbles. Her ribs are bruised. Whipped pretty hard on the backside. Kicked even. That your idea of a firm hand?"

Karl's eyes grew cold. "This horse almost killed a man once."

"I don't doubt that," Douglas replied.

"Maybe you can do better."

"Yeah, well, you don't deserve this horse or any other. We'll take her."

Douglas turned his back to Karl and led the horse away, speaking to her gently.

As Sam dealt with Karl and the rental fees, Douglas stayed with the mare in the corral. He stood near her face, rubbing her mane gently, whispering words lost to the desert winds. He maintained eye contact and never jerked his movements or appeared threatening. He knew he had to win her trust, had to join with her, had to allow her to lead herself to the saddle, after all she had been through.

Douglas rubbed her face gingerly one last time and then stepped away carefully. He turned his back to her and walked to the other end of the corral. He stood there alone, feeling the heat of the sun on his back. Douglas wondered what would happen next—if he would feel a hoof at the back of his head, a kick to his backside, or some other bit of violence.

Instead, he felt the gentle, forceful nuzzle of the mare, her hot breath just beyond his shoulder, the hair from her mane tickling his neck. He felt her power, her thunderous presence, and most important, her trust.

Theresa sat on a fence a few paces away, transfixed by what she was watching, the delicate dance between Douglas and the horse. It had been years since she had seen this kind of training—so gentle and intense—and she was surprised to see the gringo had it in him.

Leo walked up to the fence. "That's my brother, you know?" he said to her.

"You don't seem like brothers."

Leo nodded in agreement. "No, tell me about it. He's pretty good with that horse, though, ain't he?"

Theresa's gaze remained fixed on Douglas, who was now leading the mare around the corral. The horse's behavior was completely different: she followed him willingly, almost playfully. Her carriage, remarkably, had already changed, with her head held high, her posture more confident.

"I have seen this kind of training before. Very gentle. You are a policeman, too?"

"No, not me. Just Sam."

"Is he a good one?" she asked.

"I'm sure he is. He's good at everything he does. Except people."

They watched Douglas put the saddle on the mare, who now accepted it gracefully. He cinched the strap, rubbed the horse on the head and neck, and then slowly put his foot in the stirrup.

"I'm sorry about your grandfather," Leo offered.

Theresa did not respond, or maybe she couldn't without crying, and so she remained silent. Instead she focused on Douglas.

Sam walked over to join them.

"What do you think of Little Joe now?" Leo asked him.

Sam looked out at the corral and saw his little brother riding the saddled and responsive mare.

The sun was high in the western sky. Douglas rode his mare like a cowboy, effortlessly, the horse trustfully leading the way. He wore a soft wool cowboy hat with a large brim and a Mexican serape. He felt like Clint Eastwood. Theresa rode alongside him, stunningly beautiful against the vista.

Sam trailed behind them riding alone, wearing a similar hat. He scanned the horizon, looking for anything out of the ordinary. So far, all he had seen was desert and more desert.

Leo dragged, bringing up the rear. He appeared to be in some pain. He was outfitted like the others, but his coat was too heavy, the sleeves too long, and his horse was ornery and uncooperative. His hat, too big for his head, continued to slide down over his eyes, making navigation difficult.

"One size fits all, my ass," he said under his breath.

Theresa watched Douglas on his horse, leading the way. "What you did with that horse was beautiful."

"If they trust you," he said, "they teach you."

Sam moved up alongside them, looking out over the harsh terrain.

"Okay, the kidnappers gotta be talking to the FBI. There are no phone lines, and cell phones could be traced."

"Unless they were scrambled through a computer," Douglas said. "Wireless phone modems with a cell phone. E-mail."

"Hold up." Sam pulled his horse to a gentle stop. "You're gonna need a generator, and generators need gas."

"I know of only one gas depot between here and the canyons," Theresa explained.

"Can you find it?" Sam asked as Leo finally pulled up alongside the other three.

"I'm Indian," Theresa said with a heavy dose of sarcasm. "Like your cowboy movies. I get down, put my ear to the ground, smell the horse dung, sniff the wind. That's all we're good for, right?"

She rode ahead, leaving the boys behind. Her outburst was unexpected. Up until now she had remained mostly quiet, focused on the task of leading them through the landscape.

"Wow," Leo said to Sam. "What's wrong with

Hiawatha? Wake up on the wrong side of the bedroll?"

But Douglas came to her defense. "Considering what she's been through, maybe we cut her some slack, huh, Leo?" With that, he rode after her.

"Little Joe's right," Leo conceded to Sam. "It was stupid."

"Leo, you wanna know what's stupid? The *Bonanza* thing is stupid."

But the fact that Sam said it wearing a cowboy hat and perched on a horse made Leo smile. Hoss had no sense of irony.

Douglas and Theresa rode together ahead of Sam while Leo maintained his sorry and sore position at the back. The blazing sun had drifted down toward the western horizon, signaling a cooling of the day and soon the onset of dusk. Puffy white clouds could be seen gathering across the sky. Douglas stuck close to Theresa, concerned about her and her recent outburst. But her face didn't show him anything. So he tried a different tack—he started asking her questions. About anything and everything. He soon learned that she had a peculiar way of making even the bad things seem strange and interesting.

"Well, you must have cared about him once. A long time ago?"

Theresa nodded. "Edgar was like my father. He protected me from the things he knew I would not tolerate."

"You mean he lied to you?" Douglas asked.

Again she nodded. "That's what I mean. When I found out the true nature of what he did, I left. Again, like my father."

"What did your father do?"

"Verdugo worked for *him.*"

A heaviness fell between them then, as Douglas realized he didn't know Theresa very well at all. The mere thought that she could be related to the people orchestrating the mess they had gotten themselves into was beyond his reach. Luckily, Leo was there for a bit of comic relief. As he fell farther behind the others, he yelled out to them, "Hey! How do you get these things to go if they don't want to?"

They looked back to see his horse moving in circles, with Leo holding on to the reins with no guidance or precision. His hat fell over his eyes time and time again. Eventually he set the horse right, facing the same direction as the others, with the same limited vision, his hat now resting on the brim of his nose.

"The gas depot is over the next rise," Theresa said. "About a mile."

"We'll rest near here and wait till dark," Sam said, looking at the empty expanse all around them. They truly were in the middle of nowhere. Seemed to him like the perfect place to hide Wills.

Soon came the hour of the golden vista—the time of day when the landscape turned from blazing desert to beautiful panorama. The heat of the day was kept as a memory by the sand and chaparral, a small protection from the coming cold night. The sky exploded in oranges, yellows, and reds, a wide shelf of amazing color. Each in the group stared up at the sky, momentarily moved and displaced, and each took a moment alone to gather his or her thoughts as they led the horses to a nearby stream to drink.

Douglas and Leo rested in the shadow of a rock overhang near the stream. Theresa walked farther downstream, pulling the roan gently along. She removed the heavy saddle and rubbed the side of the horse. He began to graze on the patches of grass near the stream. Theresa took off her coat and bent near the stream, letting the cool water take away her fatigue. She fought back against the recurring image stuck in her head: her grandfather supine on the floor, a bouquet of red expanding grotesquely across his chest. She traced her hands through the water in the hopes of letting that terrible image be washed away in the current.

Unbeknownst to her, Leo sat nearby, transfixed by her beauty. "Now that is one gorgeous woman, ain't it?" he said to Douglas.

"Definitely."

"Tell me, little brother, how do you do it? With the ladies, I mean. Not that I need pointers or anything. Lord knows I do just fine on my own, but . . . just asking artist to artist . . . what's your technique?"

Douglas hesitated before responding. "Well, Leo, I don't really like to talk about stuff like that. It kind of kills the magic."

Leo glanced back at his brother, almost like he was hurt by the comment. "Wow. I wasn't meaning locker-room BS. I was just trying to bond, brother to brother."

Douglas looked at Leo for a beat. The "brother" thing—Leo's secret weapon for trying to get the kid to spill his guts—had hit its mark. One more push ought to get the canary singing.

"Never mind . . ." offered Leo.

Douglas dropped his saddle on the ground. "Well, the thing is," he began, "the way I get my joy, my satisfaction, depends on how intense and complete the woman's joy is. To the woman it seems very giving, because I'm acutely tuned in to her every need. But in reality, it's selfishly motivated."

Douglas went back to the horse and began unpacking his bags. Leo just stared off into the distance for a minute. "Hmmm," he said. "I guess that could work." But in truth, he had no idea what the kid was talking about.

The dark came quickly, a full moon unwavering in the desert night. Under its cover, they were now free to explore the gas depot. Sam and the others moved without sound through the hills and dirt. Even the horses were quiet, as if guessing at the covert nature of their mission.

Sam looked at the humble structure through his binoculars. The depot was nothing more than two holding tanks, about twenty feet in diameter, and two pumps. He'd seen gas stations in downtown LA with less to offer, but still.

Three armed henchmen wandered near three gas tanker trucks parked near a small, adobe building that Sam guessed functioned as an office. That was where he wanted to go.

"Leo, stay here with Theresa. Me and the kid are going to look around."

"Why do I have to stay here?" Leo asked.

"She'll protect you," Sam said.

"Ah, c'mon. Are you forgetting I'm the one that speaks Spanish?"

"I'm not going to talk to them," Sam explained. "I'm just going to look around."

"Go, Leo," Douglas said, always trying to keep the peace. "I can stay with Theresa."

"Uh, no. I think we all know where that's going."

"Don't be an idiot, Leo."

"Hey," Sam interrupted. "Listen to the kid. Starting to sound like family."

"We could all go," Theresa offered.

"No, I'm going to go alone. Less of a chance I get spotted."

"You sure about that, Sam?" asked Leo, looking at his brother's tall frame, with his dusty trench coat and his wide, white cowboy hat. "You're pretty easy to spot, especially with the neon white cowboy hat on your fat head. I wouldn't want you to get shot."

"You worried about me, Leo?"

"No. I just don't want the shot to give away our position."

Sam slipped off into the darkness.

Inside the office of the gas depot, an older hench-man named Ricardo and a younger man named Sixto plowed through the boring night shift in the only way they knew how: tequila and chess. They were well into the second bottle of the night, and the pieces on the chessboard began to waver, slowing the game down immensely. The tequila slurred their Spanish. Their coordination suffered as well.

"I'm not driving out to Pátzcuaro. It's your turn," Sixto said.

"I don't mind the drive," Ricardo commented, eyeing the board warily. He took a few moments to decide his next move. It would be easier for him to decide if the chess pieces stopped swaying.

"You play too slow for a life so short!" Sixto yelled. With that, he threw back the rest of his

tequila, got up from the table, and walked out of the office, leaving Ricardo alone.

Sam caught Sixto's exit as he snuck into the office, watching Ricardo's figure at the table start to lean forward. Soon his forehead was on the chessboard, the tequila having won the game. His heavy breathing soon turned into snoring.

Sam moved farther into the room, pushing open the door. He spied on the wall a huge map of Mexico. The area marked *Pátzcuaro* was circled in red, complete with latitude and longitude coordinates. He let out an exhale. Bingo. Sam thought they might have finally caught their first real break.

Back up the hill, the others waited for Sam beside the horses. The air had turned cold. The horses grazed on what they could find growing through the pebbles and dirt.

"Well, if you'll excuse me," Douglas said, rising from the ground. "I think this might be a good time for me to freshen up." He grabbed his backpack and headed off into the trees on the side of the hill.

"Um, be careful," Leo said, walking up to him.

"Human feces are an aphrodisiac to the Great Mexican Black Killer Grizzly." He barely contained his laugh.

"Thanks for the tip," Douglas said, brushing him off.

Theresa watched Douglas disappear into the trees. She was still thinking about his way with the horse back at the corral, his gentle training methods. "He does not have the arrogance of most men I've known."

"Well," Leo began, "he can be selfish, of course. But he's only a kid, remember."

She looked at Leo. "Your brother Sam. He seems hardened."

"Oh, yeah. That's because he is. Hardheaded, hard-nosed, hard to get along with . . ."

"But you are none of these things?" she said with a slight smile. "Hardened, selfish? Nothing like that?"

Leo couldn't help but smile. "No. No way. I'm a giver. Give, give, give, always give, never take."

"You seem very insecure," she said, as if intentionally pushing one of Leo's buttons already. The button located squarely in the middle of his forehead.

Her comment stopped Leo in his tracks.

"What? Where'd you pick that up? Some psych class at the local JC, or is that all *Dr. Phil*?"

"Who is Dr. Phil?" she asked.

Suddenly, a large knife stabbed the earth, down deep in the dirt right in front of Leo's foot. They both looked at the blade, stunned.

"You need a satellite to get *Dr. Phil* down here," said a voice from the darkness. A Mexican henchman named Octavio made his way down the incline, his AK-47 pointed right at Leo's chest. Leo hadn't heard a thing; not a rustle in the bushes or footsteps in the dirt. They'd been ambushed.

Then Theresa's head jerked back and she was pulled up off the ground from behind. Octavio's partner, Bernardo, put his knife to her throat, enveloping her in a tight grip.

Octavio kept his gun pointed squarely at Leo. He bent down to collect his knife from the dirt. "Your friends. Where they at?"

Leo sat on a rock staring up at the man with the very large gun. "What friends?" he asked, feigning innocence.

Octavio smashed Leo across the face with the butt of his AK-47. Leo slumped down against a tree, his mouth bleeding.

"The ones riding the other horses," Octavio said just before he kicked Leo in the ribs. Leo thought he heard a slight crack. But still he kept up the charade, trying to tell a different story about why they were really hiding there.

"No," he said through a mouthful of blood and a side filled with burning pain. "I'm a cow-boy. Those are my horses." He pulled a tooth out of his bloodied mouth and dropped it into the dirt. "I ride one sumbitch to death, then I got a backup."

Octavio grew angry at the gringo's obvious lies. He kicked Leo in the ribs again. This time he definitely heard a crack, and his knees momentarily left the sand.

"Tell me," Octavio threatened. "Or Bernardo cuts your girlfriend."

Leo struggled quickly to his knees, spitting blood. "No, no. I'm taking her to Verdugo. You hurt her, he'll kill all of us."

Once again Octavio was two steps ahead of him. "Verdugo is the one that sent us." With that he punched Leo, a vicious downward right with his closed, hard fist. A stream of blood and saliva flew out of his mouth, a red shooting star that fell into the sand.

"Last chance," Octavio offered. "I mean, if I kill her, she can't have my kids."

Leo looked over at Theresa, still struggling against Bernardo. His large knife glinted in the moonlight. Leo felt hopeless—he didn't know what else he could do to protect Theresa or to save himself. His side felt like it was on fire, and he was swallowing his own blood. Best to let them kill him first. At least he wouldn't have to watch anyone else die.

Just then, behind Bernardo's shoulder, Leo spied him: Douglas. Just behind his mare. Clutching a very large rock. Leo felt his strength return.

"Okay, okay," he said to Octavio. "I gave it my best shot. I'm going to be honest now: one of my friends is right behind your partner."

Octavio turned to look, and simultaneously, Douglas stepped out of the cover of night behind Bernardo and clocked him with the large rock. He went down like a sack of laundry. Leo took that moment to kick his captor right in the balls with all of his remaining strength. Octavio doubled over. Leo added a strong right cross for double measure and watched him hit the dirt as well.

"Theresa—you okay?" Douglas asked. She nodded, rubbing her neck. "Leo—you all right?" He ran to his brother, who was holding his jaw and giving off a low moan.

"I lost my tooth." He spit out blood, less of it this time. "I definitely broke a rib and my ass really hurts from that damn horse."

Douglas smiled. "But you were cool, man. Definitely cool."

"Yeah? You think? You were pretty cool, too, little brother." Leo moved to shake Douglas's hand on a job well done. Then he paused. "Whoa—you wash your hands after?"

"Always," he said.

Just then Sam walked up and all three of them jumped, their nerves still on edge from the recent attack.

Sam looked at the two unconscious thugs lying in the dirt. "Who are these guys?"

"You should've seen Leo, Sam," Douglas said, still full of adrenaline. "He wouldn't give us up!"

Leo beamed at Douglas with a gap-toothed bloody smile.

"Verdugo sent them," Theresa said, getting back to business.

"There will be more after them," Sam mused.

He turned to Theresa. "Listen, I saw on a map a town called Pátzcuaro. I've got the coordinates."

Theresa frowned. She knew that to be deep in Indian land. Which meant some of her own people were helping the Americans who were holding Wills—those who had killed her grandfather. "Pátzcuaro is half a day on horseback. Maybe one hour by truck."

"Okay. Then we go now. You guys take my horse. If that truck is leaving soon, I'm going to be on it."

Leo looked concerned. "What if we run into where they're keeping Wills? We could get him killed."

"No. The money they're asking for Wills, there's no way they get it unless they can prove he is still alive. They'll kill us first."

"How do they know we're not the FBI?" Leo asked.

"The FBI won't come in on horseback," Douglas said, shifting his hat back on his head.

Leo agreed. "That's a good point. Okay, we stick to the plan. We find Wills, call the American embassy, then go home and wait for our check."

Theresa's face blanched at the mention of

the check. "Is that all this is about for you? The money?" She practically spit out the word.

Leo had forgotten about Theresa's plight, the loss of her grandfather. He tried to backpedal and yank his foot out of his mouth. "I didn't mean it like that. I mean as long as we're here . . ."

Theresa walked away to ready the horses. "We should be ready to leave."

"I didn't mean it like that, Theresa." Even when acting like the hero of the day, Leo couldn't save his foot from flying into his mouth.

Sam looked at his brother, bloodied and prone in the dirt, and shook his head. He, too, walked away, down the hill into the darkness.

Only Douglas had a consoling word. "You meant well."

Leo ran his finger through the dirt. From hero to zero in less than a minute. Even for him it was a personal record.

Chapter
TWENTY-THREE

Daybreak found Nealon holding his gun, checking the ammunition, and slipping it into the holder. He peered out the window and surveyed the perimeter of the compound. All seemed quiet. The heat of the morning baked the air, and even the dirt was still. The ranch looked deserted, even though Nealon knew his men, armed and just a bit dangerous, were at the ready nearby. The only movement came from the incessant talking of Canton, who was fumbling with his laptop and checking their other equipment. The entire plan rested on that laptop—a not insignificant piece of machinery.

Canton continued to drone on. "I had a

dream last night the guys who killed Rodriguez, whoever they are, were just a myth."

Nealon paid him little attention, as usual, and continued filling his backpack. It was almost time to leave. To get the transfers, ditch Wills, and get the hell out of this overheated rattrap.

"I dreamed you orchestrated the whole thing so we wouldn't have to split the money."

Canton's insight drew a smile from Nealon. Again he wondered if Canton knew the thin ice he was walking over. "I'm not that clever," Nealon said.

"Don't underestimate yourself."

Nealon took a seat with his gun in hand and stared at Canton. His trigger finger started to itch. Canton went back to fiddling with a fried motherboard he'd removed from one of the other laptops. Yup. Thin ice indeed.

A few miles away, on yet another thin dirt road, a flatbed truck roared past the desert chaparral on its way to the compound.

Four red gas cylinders were bolted to the flatbed. A gas pump attachment was also held fast in the back of the truck next to a tarp covering a large, lumpy package. Mexican radio played, the only station for miles, and offered the single distraction from the endless earth and heat.

Sam lay still underneath the tarp, his back against the floor of the flatbed. It had been a rough trip trapped under the heat of the tarp as the sun baked its surface. His body was sore, having had to keep still during the early-morning drive. Each bump and hole in the road felt like a punch in his gut or lower back. His legs were stiff, their muscles tightening. He felt like he had just gone five rounds in the ring.

Sam shed the tarp around him and moved it to the side of the flatbed. He surveyed the area all around him: nothing but desert brush and flat vistas. He cracked his neck and kept as low as he could, whisking one leg over the stake rails of the flatbed truck, and then the other.

Hot wind blew against his face, and Sam inched toward the passenger-side door. With a firm grip on the wooden flats across the side of the truck, Sam peered in to see the two men from the gas depot singing along to the radio, their faces placid and weathered. Ricardo was behind the wheel, with Sixto heavy and dull by his side. Sam noticed the door was unlocked.

Sam leaned over and lifted the door handle of the truck. Before Sixto could react, Sam's meaty fist came flying through the open space, hitting him square in the face. His hat fell to the floor. Sam grabbed him by the collar and in one fluid motion yanked Sixto out of the seat and out of the truck. His cold-cocked body fell with a thud into the passing brush and dirt while Ricardo, still lost in song like the first week's loser in *American Idol,* continued his rendition of "Cielito Lindo."

Sam leaped into the cab of the truck and pulled out the piece he took from the armory. It happened so quickly that Ricardo didn't even have time to react until he was staring down the barrel of the gun. Sam's face was solid steel, his eyes taking aim along with the gun.

"Habla ingles?" Sam asked.

Ricardo's eyes were as wide as wheels. "Not much. *Un poco.*"

"You understand you *habla* too much I'll kill you?"

Ricardo understood, more from the gun in his face than Sam's words. *"Sí."*

"Good," Sam said, settling into the passenger seat. He picked up Sixto's dropped hat and placed it on his head. He kept his gun firmly set on Ricardo, whose trembling figure and matchstick arms didn't seem to pose much of a threat. The Mexican radio sang on, its tinny music echoing across the vista.

Sam set his eyes on the road ahead. In a short time, he guessed, they'd arrive at the compound. There was no doubt in his mind that Wills's captors would put up a more difficult fight than these two drunks. Sam rechecked the odds in his head. It was one man, one gun, going up against an entire compound of men loaded to the teeth with automatic rifles and God knows what else.

Sam figured it was as fair a fight as he was going to find.

Chapter
TWENTY-FOUR

Kyle Wills dreamed of cool, blue water, crystal-clear and inviting. He sat by the wide tiled swimming pool in his spacious, landscaped backyard. The grass was the color of money and trimmed like a crew cut. The trees were high and shading, not an errant leaf among them. The surface of the pool was calm and shining, like glass. The path to the water was made of flagstone, rustic yet elegant, imported from a country he could no longer recall. It was his wife who insisted on building this little oasis in the middle of their lives, a perfectly secluded spot behind their mansion in the middle of a big city. Sitting here, he felt like he was light-years away from everything.

Kyle watched his wife and son beckon to him from the other side of the pool. He was hot—he was parched, in fact—and nothing would feel better than to go to them and jump into the cool, enticing water.

Wills rose from the chaise lounge. His feet felt the soft flagstone beneath him, warm to the touch. But he couldn't move. He willed his body to walk toward them, but it wouldn't respond. He looked across the pool to his wife, who was now crying, her face melting into huge, racking sobs. But his son, Janson, didn't seem to notice. He just stared at his father, his face unmoving, his eyes cold.

"What do you do, Dad?" Janson asked. "What do you actually do?"

At that moment, Wills looked down at his feet that wouldn't budge. There he could see the metal shackles around his ankles, the heavy chains wrapped around his legs, keeping him in place.

A sharp, loud voice woke him from the dream. Wills cracked open his eyes and immediately felt the sandpaper in his throat. It was so dry, he could barely swallow. He looked over and saw Canton in the room, laptop in hand.

"Rise and shine, pumpkin head. That's what my mother used to say." His voice cut through the stale, hot air of the cabin as he once again set up the computer system they had been using to communicate with the FBI. Wills stared at the round man, once again resigned. The dream of his family had taken the last bit of hope he had left. He was, most likely, a dead man.

"If all goes as planned," Canton continued, his fingers flying across the keypad, "you should be back with your pseudo–loved ones by happy hour tomorrow night. At which point I will be halfway to handsome."

Wills didn't move. It was as if his entire body were chained to the cot, not just his ankle. It hurt to speak. "Before you do whatever it is you've planned, will I be able to talk to my son?"

Canton gave the desperate man a smirk. "You're pretty sure we're going to kill you, huh?"

"It's crossed my mind."

"Well, you're wrong—again. You took fifty million dollars from me, I take five hundred million from you. Which is what I would have had if I invested the fifty mil in the first place. Swear to God. An eye for an eye. It's biblical, man."

Wills tried to wrap his mind around the

words, to see if perhaps he was telling the truth. If perhaps this was not the end.

Just then Nealon walked into the room, his tall body casting a grotesque shadow on the floor of the cabin. Canton hardly noticed him, focused instead on the laptop in front of him. Nealon looked around the room, a scowl growing on his face.

"You said a few minutes, goddamn it!"

"It's only been a few minutes," Canton replied. "What's the matter, is the 'Iceman' having a meltdown?"

There was a pause as the screen in front of Canton refreshed and uploaded. Suddenly, the monitor lit up, his face caught in the blue glow. The monitor showed a global network of newly established bank accounts, each ready for a deposit from the very scared and beaten billionaire currently chained to the floor.

Canton snapped his fingers excitedly. "Got it! I got it, baby! I'm all set up for the transfer. Now we put our buddy here online and the party gets started."

Canton moved over to the laptop in front of Wills and fired it up to bring their prisoner online. Then he rushed back to his own laptop, pushing Nealon aside. His fingers flew over the keyboard as the screen continued to glow. "Here we go," he said.

Wills sat still on the cot, staring at his reflection in the laptop screen. A small twinge of hope returned to him—that this would soon be over, that he might live through it, that money, indeed, could buy him anything at all, even his own freedom.

Outside, he could hear the rattle of an arriving truck pulling up to the compound.

Chapter
TWENTY-FIVE

Sam eyed the stone cabins and different out-buildings of the compound as Ricardo drove the gas truck into the belly of the beast. The driver pulled up a few feet in front of the compound's main building, off to the side near the brush, and went back to the flatbed. Ricardo stood by the bumper, waiting for instructions on which vehicles needed gas.

Sam leaned on the hood of the truck, pulling the hat down low over his eyes, and watched the activity from his shaded vantage point. It was an old cop trick: hiding in plain sight to get the lay of the land. Sam watched a handful of armed men come out of the woodwork, their guns glinting in the sunlight. They seemed to gravitate toward one building in the center of the compound—no one had gone inside the stone cabin, but there were always a few armed men lingering in front of it—and his instincts told him this was where they were keeping Wills.

He watched a few Jeeps appear from behind the stone cabin—more targets he'd have to contend with. He figured the only thing standing between him and Wills was maybe eight men and a boatload of ammunition, all of which could cut him down before he even got a running start.

Sam didn't like the odds. He needed backup. He needed his brothers.

Just south of the perimeter, on the edge of a hill behind a cover of rocks, Leo Carey had his eyes on the entire situation. Through his binoculars, he surveyed the compound and noticed the number of men with guns. He watched the truck pull into the compound, its red barrels of gasoline reflecting the strong sun overhead. From the hill, behind the brush, he could see everything. He watched the driver of the truck get out, a spooked look on his face. Then he saw a more familiar figure, in a dark cowboy hat.

"Sam just pulled up in the gas truck. Pretty sure he's the one in the dorky cowboy hat with the King Kong shoulders."

He gave the binoculars to Douglas.

"See him?" Leo asked.

"Yup," Douglas replied. But what he noticed more was the number of men hovering around the gas truck, each armed with a rifle or automatic weapon, and a few Jeeps arriving from the other side of the stone cabin.

And there was Sam, pathetically outgunned, stuck in the middle of it all.

They moved the horses over to the base of the hill. Theresa held the reins while Douglas and Leo, rifles in hand, crawled to their position on top of the hill.

Sam pretended to stand guard at the hood of the gas truck. He watched Bermutti, the explosives expert, pull up behind them in a bright orange Jeep. Bertram also came forward, motioning another Jeep, gun-metal gray with patches of rust over its hood, into line. He yelled to Ricardo in Spanish.

"The two Jeeps first," he said. Ricardo nodded

and went to the back of the flatbed to grab the gas pump.

Bertram and Bermutti stood close by, watching Ricardo move the pump toward the Jeeps, not noticing the large man on the other side of the gas truck in the black hat pull a small, military-grade grenade from his coat pocket. Sam held the explosive device in his meaty hand. The pin glittered in the sunlight.

Inside the stone cabin, Canton continued to work his magic over the keyboard of his laptop. The screen showed the numbers rolling into their main offshore account. Nealon was breathing down his neck; his breath smelled of tobacco and something else, something rank.

Wills sat in place, still chained to the floor, reading stock quotes off the ticker running across the bottom of the monitor that held the picture of his wife and Janson, watching on the other end of the line.

AOL down four and an eighth, GE down a half, Cisco's down two and change . . .

Canton punched a few more buttons to try and activate the transfer. He once again felt

Nealon's breath on his neck. "Can you back the hell off, please! I can't even think here."

Wills stared at the image of his son sitting by his mother. The young boy's face was no different from the one he'd seen in his dream. Only this time the boy let loose a small stream of tears. The image broke what was left of Wills's heart. He stopped reading the stock figures and addressed his son directly.

"Janson," Wills said, his voice raspy.

His eyes lit up. "Yeah, Dad?"

"I wanted to tell you what I do for a living. For your report."

But it was too late. "I turned it in, Dad," Janson said. "I made some stuff up."

Wills let out a long breath. "I'm sorry."

Janson shrugged his slight shoulders. "But I'd still like to know."

Canton, working too feverishly on the computer to notice the interaction between father and son, finally got the account transactions to go through. He watched the lights as the money moved across the globe, the entire world at his fingertips. The transfer was complete: 500 million dollars.

"Got it! Son of a bitch!" he yelled, not yet able

to process the sheer amount of money now in his possession. "Now I split it up and we're out of here."

Wills stared at his son's face. He looked so scared. His wife, too. He had no idea how to reassure them both that the money was being transferred as they spoke and that, soon, they would all be together once again. Safe once again.

He was just about to speak, to try and comfort them, when they all heard the explosion.

Chapter
TWENTY-SIX

With his back to Bertram, Bermutti, and the other henchmen, Sam pulled the silver pin out of the grenade and lobbed it out into the desert a few feet beyond the gas truck. It exploded in a shower of dirt and dust raining down on them.

The explosion rocked the entire compound like a beehive that had just been kicked. Men came running, guns drawn. Bermutti pulled his piece and crouched down low behind the orange Jeep for cover. Bertram did the same, drawing out his handgun and leaning against the front tire of the gray Jeep. Even Ricardo, now visibly shaking, opened the truck door and crawled inside below the passenger seat, cowering in the footwell of the truck.

"Good God, Sam, are you out of your mind?" Leo said, grabbing Douglas by the arm and pulling him down the mountain back toward Theresa and the horses.

Taking advantage of the confusion and panic caused by Sam's unexpected grenade, Leo, Douglas, and Theresa huddled together, out of sight from the compound deep in a ravine.

"We gotta split up and haul ass," Leo whispered. "Make 'em think there's more of us."

Bermutti stayed low near the orange Jeep, frantically surveying the compound. He couldn't see a thing. He motioned to the other henchmen, who likewise shrugged. He could tell from the size and sound of the explosion that it was a grenade, probably military grade. The only one in these parts who had such weaponry was Verdugo, but stealth wasn't his style. If Verdugo was behind this attack, they'd be dead already.

Bertram stayed down in a cover position behind the gray Jeep, compacted in the dirt near the front wheel. He had no idea what was happening. They were being attacked, but by who? No one even knew they were out here.

"Anybody see anything?" Bertram yelled to the others.

"I see the future," a voice said. "And you're not in it."

Bertram felt Sam before he could hear him, the large boot displacing the dirt and casting a shadow across the ground. The metal felt cool to his enraged temple. Bertram stayed calm; it wasn't the first time he'd had a gun to his head.

Sam muscled Bertram up from the ground, from the safety of the Jeep. He was careful to keep Bertram in front of him, using the man as a shield against the others around the courtyard in front of the main house.

"Where's Wills?" Sam asked him.

"Dead. You're late."

"If he was dead, you would've moved on by now."

Sam led Bertram forward, the gun at the side of his neck. Out in the open, everyone could see the large man with the dark hat holding a gun to Bertram's head. But there was no clear shot as Sam continued to use the killer as a shield. He had no way of knowing this was the man who had killed Theresa's grandfather and, if given the chance, would do the same thing to him.

But Theresa noticed him as she and Douglas made their way covertly into the compound; the other henchmen kept their focus on Sam and his captive. Her eyes narrowed when she saw Bertram. "The one with Sam killed my grandfather," she said to Douglas. He narrowed his focus as well before they split apart, each moving into position to provide backup for Sam.

The compound now had the appearance of high noon—a traditional standoff. Suddenly, Nealon emerged from the stone cabin, his tall frame bounding out of the doorway and down the front steps. He held a nine millimeter in front of him, pointed at Sam, not seeming to care that his hired killer might be in the pathway of the bullet.

"You must be the guy that killed Rodriguez," Nealon said. They formed a Mexican standoff, Nealon locking eyes with Sam. All guns were trained on Sam and Bertram, the heat of the afternoon intensifying the tension and anxiety of the standoff. Bertram tried to make eye contact with Nealon, but the man just wouldn't do it. Bertram shook his head, his eyes losing hope that any of this would end well for him.

"You picked the wrong horse, Bubba," he said under his breath to Sam.

Nealon smiled and then shrugged. "Kill them

both," he said to the collection of guns around them.

Nealon's words seemed to stop time as they hung there in the hot air of the Mexican desert. But before any of the henchmen could pull the triggers of their weapons, they were met with a shower of bullets seemingly from out of nowhere. Sam's backup had finally arrived and kicked into high gear.

Leo, Douglas, and Theresa, all from different points surrounding the compound, took aim and opened fire.

Douglas aimed for the henchman closest to Sam. He pulled the rifle's trigger and the man went down, taking a bullet right to the gut in a spray of blood and air. Bermutti then took aim at Sam, trying to free his friend from the standoff. His shot went wide and grazed Sam's arm, but it was enough to get Bertram free. So Bermutti fired another shot as he took cover once again on the other side of his orange Jeep. Nealon sprinted back into the safety of the stone cabin, if only to avoid all the bullets and check on the money transfers. Sam wavered to get to the back of the Jeep as Bertram ducked low to the ground, beneath the firestorm that was now all around them. Leo, Douglas, and Theresa were letting loose a steady stream of fire. The henchmen, mostly Indian, fired back, keeping the three shooters from advancing closer to the compound and the now injured Sam.

One henchman with a machine gun climbed the steps of the stone cabin before Leo took him out. Another tried the same, but Theresa shot him square in the chest. She'd had her eyes trained on Bertram, the one who killed her grandfather, but in the chaos caused by the explosion and the gunfight she had lost sight of him.

From just beyond the main center of the compound, Douglas, staying low, made his way behind a group of cacti and scrub brush. Through the weeds he could just see the orange Jeep. He pulled a grenade from his pocket and pulled the pin. He lobbed the bomb over the brush and took cover.

The grenade landed in the dirt with a small thud, right under the carriage of the orange Jeep. Bermutti, crouched down near the rear wheel, heard the minute sound. Instantly, his senses were alert. He spied the grenade almost squarely under the Jeep. His eyes grew wide. So he was right. It was a military grenade after all.

The second explosion matched the first, only this time there was a Jeep to add to the intensity of the destruction. The explosion ripped into the metal framework and wheels in a firestorm, sending it airborne. Bermutti, the onetime explosives expert, barely had time to breathe the hot air before he was engulfed in flames, his dead, ruined body thrown backward from the momentum of the blast. The Jeep, now a flaming, twisted ruin, landed back on the ground, upside down, flames shooting into an already heated sky.

Chapter
TWENTY-SEVEN

It sounded like a war zone. One minute Wills was speaking with his family, oppressed by the quiet of the stone cabin, and the next there was an explosion. Instinct told him to duck and cover, but he couldn't move, his hands bound and his feet chained to the floor. He saw Nealon leave and, through the walls of the cabin, heard him say "Kill them both" before coming back inside. And then more mayhem, more explosions. He could hear the bloodshed occurring outside.

Canton was similarly unnerved. He remained at his keypad and continued to type furiously, the rapid keyboard sounding, too, like gunfire. His monitor showed the money being split into accounts located in various places around the world: the Caribbean, Switzerland, Tokyo, and Moscow. Beads of sweat formed on his forehead with each new volley of gunfire he heard from outside. He had to finish—he had to get the money separated and dispersed so they could get the hell out of there.

Trying to block out the gunfight in front of the compound, Wills fought to maintain composure. The feed to his family was still live, and they could still see him through the laptop. Janson's eyes showed nothing but fear; his wife was similarly terrified, clutching their son tightly. He had to remain calm. He had to pretend, for their sakes, that everything would work out safely.

Wills returned to the conversation they were having before the explosion. His son wanted to know about business. He knew about business. He could keep talking to distract them from the danger, from the fact that at any moment a bullet could come through the window and end his life.

"It all starts with an idea, right?" Wills began. "Some people come up with ideas. Good people, good ideas. That's how you start a business. And that's what my company does."

Canton, overseeing the exchanges online,

couldn't help but hear Wills talking to his son. Of course it was pure bullshit. Despite the fact that he was scared out of his mind, he couldn't let the crooked billionaire get away with this. Not with this. Not when the man had stolen Canton's very own company out from underneath him. Upended his life and put him through hell.

As he continued to type furiously, he yelled a single word. "Bullshit!"

Done! With the transfers complete, Canton grabbed his laptop and shoved it into his backpack. He ran over to Wills, who was still talking to his son.

"You almost make it sound like charity work, you puke!" Canton stuck his terrified face into the sight line of the laptop's camera. "Yeah, kid. Then your old man fires all the people and brings in teams of lawyers and private investigators to ruin everybody's lives. Trust me, I know from firsthand experience! That's what your old man does."

With his backpack in hand, Canton sprinted out of the room, leaving the accusation hanging in the air. Wills could only stare at the sight of his son's face as he realized what kind of business his father ran, what he actually did. The reasons behind his distance, the secrets, the gunfire, the explosions, even this entire kidnapping. They all stemmed from what his father and his company did.

Wills had no defense.

"Do you do that, Dad?" Janson asked, his voice thin and barely audible.

Wills just stared back at his son, not knowing what to say. There was nothing left to say. Nothing but the truth.

"Yes," Wills admitted with a catch in his throat. "That's what I do."

Outside, the sound of gunfire continued.

Chapter
TWENTY-EIGHT

Sam kneeled in the hard dirt, holding his arm. Blood had soaked through the entire sleeve of his coat, but the burning had ended. The bleeding had slowed down as well. It was a clean shot; the bullet went straight into the meat of his arm and out again. And although it hurt like a bitch, Sam still had use of the arm. He wiped the drying blood on his jeans and tried to survey what had happened and who else was left. He knew the leader was inside the stone cabin, along with a few others and probably Wills. His brothers had remained on the perimeter to keep the gunfire coming, their positions concealing the fact that there were only four of them leading the assault. He crouched down lower in the dirt, flexing his fist to keep the feeling in his hand.

Out of the corner of his eye he saw Bertram, the one he tried to use as a shield, sneak up on his far left flank. He raised his gun toward Sam, but just then two shots from Leo's rifle struck near him, sending Bertram back around to the side of a large black Bronco for cover. Sam fired toward him as well, hoping for a better shot from his angle. He managed to hit only the truck, which now sported bullet holes along its side and rear bumper.

Into the gunfight came Nealon and Canton, rushing out the side door of the cabin. Nealon was throwing cover fire toward the brush, hoping to catch one of the shooters' locations. Canton was cradling his backpack, protecting the laptop that held the money transfer information. Douglas and Theresa aimed at them, scattering the stone and dirt around them, to no avail. Both Canton and Nealon jumped into a waiting pickup truck. Leo joined in, spitting bullets from his rifle. He shattered the back window of the truck, but it did not stop their escape.

Bertram, still pinned on the other side of the black Bronco, heard the gunfire as well as Nealon making his escape. He opened the passenger-side door and jumped in, just as Sam got a bead on him. Sam's bullet demolished the passenger-side window, but Bertram was already inside. He stayed low, floored the gas, and pulled the truck away from the gunfight. He headed away from the compound, down a dusty dirt road, toward freedom, in the opposite direction Nealon and Canton were headed.

Suddenly, the air was quiet. No more gunfire, no more explosions. Sam stood up and watched the trucks speeding away. They had missed their shot. They had failed. The perps were getting away. And there wasn't a damn thing Sam could do to stop them.

The pounding on the dirt was faint at first, a muted drumbeat that then roared to life. Sam heard a whistle. He turned to see Douglas charging hard on his faithful palomino, pulling Sam's horse in tow. Sam ran to his side, and Douglas handed him the reins.

"Theresa and Leo will check the grounds for Wills. I'm going after the Bronco. Theresa says there is a pass through the mountains."

But Sam was confused. "The Bronco doesn't matter."

"It matters to Theresa," Douglas explained. "That guy killed her grandfather."

Sam nodded. He understood. He thought back to his face frozen on the television monitor in Captain Haymer's office. Felt like years ago. But Sam understood. He understood the need to set things right. And so he nodded to Douglas.

"Don't get hurt, kid."

Douglas pulled the reins of the palomino tight and like a flash of lightning took off in the direction of the setting sun, a cloud of dirt and ambition trailing behind him.

Sam jumped up on his horse. From that vantage point, he surveyed the damage. A few bodies lay still in the dirt. The orange Jeep lay upside down, fire still raging from its carriage. Sam could see the truck carrying Nealon getting smaller in the distance. He stuck his heels into the horse's sides and off they went, hoping to close the distance between them and the pickup truck.

Leo, still a safe distance from the fire and hidden by the brush, pulled out his cell phone and dialed. He watched one brother head in one direction, and his other brother the opposite way. He still didn't understand the vendetta they both carried. Sure, he wanted to help Theresa as much as she had helped them, but he knew when to call a fight. They had just lived through two explosions and the biggest armed showdown since the Alamo, and the four of them actually forced an entire squad of well-armed kidnappers to make a hasty retreat. As far as he was concerned, the only thing left to do was collect the reward money and call it a day. They were lucky to be alive, let alone rich and alive. Couldn't his other brothers see that this thing was now over?

He heard the familiar click in his ear and then spoke quickly in Spanish.

"I need the number of the American embassy in Mexico City. Can you hear me?" The reception was terrible there in the middle of the desolate desert, the call fading in and out. He moved two feet to his left. *"Can you hear me now?"*

The roar in his ear had nothing to do with terrible cell phone service. It was deeper, more severe, and, worse, it was all around him. He looked off in the distance and there he saw it: a convoy of black, shining Humvees. Full of men. Heavily armed men, no doubt.

"Verdugo," Leo said under his breath.

Verdugo sat in the comfort of the Humvee, shielded from the harsh sunlight and smell of burning metal that filled the air around the compound. While he was in a distasteful line of work, Verdugo still had taste: fine tequila, an appreciation of art, and a great, great passion for timing. From what his men learned at the gas depot, before they were brutally beaten by the Americans, of course Pátzcuaro would be the perfect place to hide the billionaire. He only had to wait for the Americans to make their move. He had placed the call to the embassy earlier, and now all he had to do was tiptoe through the carnage, pick out Wills, and collect the handsome reward. It was the thing he loved most about his work: the ability to profit off other people's hard labor.

The Humvees traveled up the single-lane dirt road leading to the compound. They maneuvered gracefully around the burning Jeep and the dead bodies. Verdugo, stylishly dressed in

Armani casuals, barely gave the bodies a second glance as he crossed over the messy path and up the steps to the stone cabin.

Verdugo's bodyguards entered the house with guns drawn, eyeing Wills from behind dark sunglasses. Wills raised his bound hands as best he could, wondering what hell was to come next. Once the two large men ascertained that no one else was in the room, they nodded to the doorway.

Verdugo walked into the room, looking around the shabby accommodations with disdain. The smell of burning rubber and blood was thick in the air. He didn't like to expose himself to such unpleasantness, but this was a special situation. One he needed to take care of himself.

Verdugo looked at the beaten-down man dressed in dirtied, tattered clothing. His face told a story: of violence, hunger, fear, deprivation, and, worse, regret.

"Señor Wills?" Verdugo asked.

The prisoner nodded. Verdugo crossed over to him. He grabbed the man's hands only to find they were bound in handcuffs.

"Ah, *mira*. This is unacceptable."

Wills looked confused.

"Are you with the FBI?" he asked.

Verdugo only smiled. "No, no. I am here to escort you to them. You are safe now. You're in safe hands," he said, placing his own hand on Wills's shoulder.

Chapter
TWENTY-NINE

The wide vista was breathtaking in the late-afternoon light: a wide shelf of earth and air. Douglas rode the horizon line hard, and it felt like flying. His horse was strong underneath him, pounding the dirt with each stride forward, enjoying the freedom to just run as hard and as fast as she could. They crested a hill as fluid as a wave, sunlight dappling the rock formations and their fingerlike shadows and the purple-hued mountains in the distance. Douglas took a deep breath and spied, across a wide field of dirt and brush, the Bronco raging east in a cloud of sand and dust. He trained the white mare on it, and then they were off again, rumbling over the hard-packed desert, eager to cut off the truck and, more important, the man behind its wheel. The man who had killed Theresa's grandfather.

Scoping down the side of the hill, Douglas watched the Bronco cut across the valley and accelerate up the incline. There was too much distance between them, and the Bronco, at that speed, was pulling away too quickly; they could never catch up. Douglas needed to level the playing field.

He leaned down close to the horse that, even foaming at her mouth, was ready to go. He spoke into her ear, rubbing her along the neck.

"I know before they beat you, you had it in you. Now you show me. C'mon, let's go!"

The horse took off like a rocket, moving so fast they barely cast a shadow on the parched, cracked earth. Douglas remembered Theresa's advice and followed her directions to a pass in the hills, one the Bronco couldn't have seen or known about. This was Indian land after all, and no one knew the terrain better than Theresa.

Douglas and the palomino disappeared over the horizon. He hoped they would be fast enough to bring her some justice, bring her some peace.

• • •

The Bronco bounded over the bumpy road, covered in dirt and bullet holes. Bertram's hands were white-knuckled on the wheel. The sun was setting quickly, and soon he would not be able to make out the road and all of its twists and turns. He doubted the headlights still worked after being shot out at the compound. The side of the truck was riddled with bullet holes. He was lucky to still be intact.

He looked nervously in his rearview mirror for the kid and the white horse. They gave quite a chase, Bertram had to admit, but no horse was a match for a car. They would choke on the dust left in his wake. He pushed the gas pedal farther to the ground, increasing the Bronco's speed. The tires slid across the dirt as Bertram made a hard right, turning around the base of a large hill. He could see the scrub brush up the side of the hill, a cactus or two dotting the incline.

He looked once again in his rearview mirror and saw nothing. He started to smile.

Bertram followed the road around the base of the hill. Coming off a blind turn Bertram could see the pillars of mountains around him, the gravel road becoming thicker now, without as much sand.

He looked again in his rearview mirror and saw nothing.

Bertram turned his gaze back to the road in front of him, and there they were: the kid on the white horse.

Douglas sat patiently on the strong palomino, his hand resting on the saddle, his rifle, cocked and reloaded, poised across his forearm. He shut one eye and took aim. He unleashed a stream of bullets into the oncoming Bronco. It felt to Douglas like target practice. The hail of ammunition made spiderwebs out of the windshield and riddled the hood with ragged holes.

Douglas watched the truck sway from side to side before leaning toward the right side of the road, at full speed, and catching air. The Bronco turned on its side and skidded passenger side up for a few feet before flipping over entirely. Its forward motion carried the truck through the full flip and right side up again before coming to a hard bounce on the dirt road. Bertram collapsed out of the driver's side like a bleeding toy surprise, his body lying supine in the dust.

Douglas sat motionless on the horse, watching the wreck about twenty feet in front of him. He saw Bertram lying on his back on the ground, still as a coffin. Douglas dismounted and walked slowly toward the truck. Toward the body.

Bertram didn't move. Blood covered the side of his head, making his skin look pale and gray. He had landed on a small lump of dirt and so his chest protruded forward and his head was cast back, as if something beneath him was trying to drill through his chest.

Douglas stood over the body, rifle in hand. He had never killed anyone at close range before. Barely ever punched a man. And before he had met his two brothers and gone on this adventure, he had never even seen a dead body up close before. Its shape, like badly folded laundry, and how quickly the color departs and leaves the skin gray. Douglas nudged the body with his boot, just in case. Still no movement.

Douglas stood and tried to catch his breath. His hands were shaking a little. And even though he knew what this man had done to Theresa's grandfather, he still felt a little sorry for him. No one deserves to die alone in the desert.

The thought had barely finished forming in his head when the body lunged at him.

Bertram raised his hand and plunged a knife right into Douglas's leg, as if he were setting up stakes in it, deep into the meat of his thigh. Douglas dropped his rifle and screamed out in pain as blood instantly spurted from the wound, almost turning the dust around his boots into mud.

Douglas staggered back and collapsed on the ground, reaching for the knife handle sticking out of his leg. He watched Bertram pull himself up from the ground using the side of the ruined truck. A tire iron was in his hand, and Bertram found the strength to lift it over his head, ready to bash Douglas's head in. Ready to strike a killing blow to Douglas's injured body.

Bertram looked like a monster, bruised, eyes full of rage, head covered in blood, tire iron poised to strike above his head as he moved toward Douglas on the ground. But he moved like an unsteady bookcase, ready to topple over with the wrong distribution of weight.

Douglas summoned the last of his will to kick Bertram as hard as he could in the left leg. The leg buckled out from underneath the weakened Bertram but his momentum caused him to fall forward, the tire iron headed for Douglas's skull. In one fast motion, Douglas wrenched the knife out of his leg and in the split second before Bertram's tire iron met its mark, Douglas twisted hard to his right, then reached back and plunged the knife deep into the middle of Bertram's back.

Bertram gave a twitch and a moan. His eyes stayed open and his lips spread into the dirt.

Douglas pushed himself away from the body and the truck, trying to get out of the blood now all around them. His leg was on fire—it sent rockets of pain shooting up and down his body. It hurt to move, to breathe, to think.

The thought occurred to him once again that no one deserves to die alone in the desert, most of all, him.

He thought of Theresa—that at least she might find some peace now that her grandfather's murder had been avenged. He thought of everything that had happened over the last few days: leaving Folsom, eager for his freedom in the real world; seeing Allie again, her long legs clicking a song across the parking lot; the letter from Nina and learning that he not only had a father but siblings as well. And he thought of his two brothers, how eager and happy he had been to meet them, have a beer, even watch them fight.

And as his head fell back in the dirt and the sun set in the desert and the stars came out to play, he thought what a shame it was, now that he'd found them, that it was time for him to leave.

Chapter
THIRTY

He felt the cool night air running over his face. His throat was dry and parched. His hands were cold, and that was the third thing he noticed.

His vision blurry, he thought he saw the face of an angel with long, dark hair wearing a leather coat. She looked at him with deep, serious eyes. She was wrapping a bandage around his leg, tying the knot tight.

He winced from the pain. If he was dead, how come he could still feel pain? And why was he hearing Leo's voice in his ear?

"You lost a lot of blood there, Little Joe."

Douglas's vision cleared to find Leo, Sam, and Theresa hovering over him. He lay in the dirt near the crash. He'd made it, after all.

"You okay, kid?" Sam asked.

Douglas kept his bandaged leg still but turned his head to face his brother.

"Hey, Sam. You find Wills?"

Theresa answered for him. "Verdugo came and turned him over to the FBI like a Good Samaritan."

He leaned up, lifting his back from the dirt and getting into a sitting position. His head was clear again. "What does that mean for us?"

"It means we're broke," Leo said. "I gotta admit, though . . . seeing that asshole tits up was worth a million bucks." He was referring to Bertram, whose body still lay by the side of the road. Leo nudged Theresa, as if to commiserate in the joy of having achieved vengeance for her grandfather's murder.

But Theresa obviously didn't agree with him. "Unfortunately, it doesn't bring my grandfather back, does it?" Her words were laced with sadness, as if seeing another dead body brought back painful memories for her. She rose and walked off toward the horses waiting nearby. She cut a sad, solitary figure in the moonlight.

Leo watched her go, shaking his head. "I can't catch a break with this broad, can I?" he said quietly.

"Try keeping your mouth shut," Sam offered.

Douglas reached out to Leo, who helped him up off the ground. Douglas leaned on his brother until he regained his balance.

"I got to admit, Leo. It would save you a lot of problems," he said before hobbling away on one leg.

Not far away, in a wooded area deeper in the desert, Nealon and Canton made their way through the night. Backpacks in hand, they followed behind two Indian guides, both carrying automatic rifles over their shoulders. They were still on Indian land, and Nealon had paid a high price to get these guides to see them through the woods and into the canyons.

They moved quickly through the dense, dark terrain, trying to keep up with the Indians. Both men were breathing hard, exhausted after the day of gunfights, explosions, extortion, and kidnapping. Canton especially was pulling up the rear, having spent more of his life behind a computer than out getting exercise. His large frame was not used to such physical exertion. Finally, he couldn't take any more running.

"Wait . . . wait a minute!" he yelled, completely out of breath. "I didn't come all this way to die from exhaustion. Give me five minutes."

Without waiting for permission from the others, Canton stopped and sat on a nearby rock. He removed his heavy backpack and placed it on the rock next to him.

Nealon looked back at him and shook his head. "Well, I guess this is as good a place as any." The guides understood and kept their distance, moving over to a group of trees to wait for their leader's signal.

Nealon walked over to Canton, who was still trying to catch his breath. He picked up the pack from the rock. Canton lunged for it and only caught air.

"Get out of my stuff!" Canton yelled.

Nealon shoved him to the ground with one push. Canton lay on his back in the dirt. Before he could get back up, the Indian guides were on him, pointing their rifles at his chest. The smell of a double cross was in the air.

"Ah, c'mon, guys, put those down," Canton said, as if they might lower their weapons due to his words alone.

Nealon opened the backpack and rooted

around inside. He pulled out a flash drive no bigger than the tip of a switchblade. It glowed in the moonlight.

"Is this the backup?" he asked. "The backup flash drive, is that what this is?"

Canton panicked, keeping one eye on the rifles and one eye on Nealon. "Of course that's it. That's all we need. C'mon, let's get going."

Nealon zipped the backpack shut. Then he smashed it repeatedly over the large rock. Canton could hear the laptop inside breaking into pieces. It was the sound of his future disappearing.

"What are you doing?" he yelled. "Are you insane?" Canton jumped up and charged at Nealon, who easily pushed him back down again. Canton's ass hit the dirt hard.

"Sit down," Nealon yelled. "You're pathetic."

With that Nealon pulled out a gun from behind his back and pointed it at Canton. The fat man lay on the ground, terrified. He watched Nealon's face turn to ice—as it always did before a killing.

"You were right," Nealon said. "I underestimated myself."

Canton was almost too stunned to speak. "Why didn't I see this?"

"Stop talking," Nealon said, the gun in his hand steady and hard.

"Please," Canton begged. "Tell my mother . . ."

Nealon didn't even wait for him to finish. He fired the gun at close range, killing Canton in cold blood. The Iceman always killed in cold blood.

The sound of the gunshot carried through the trees and the canyons. As they walked, miles away from the scene, Sam, Theresa, Leo, and Douglas could hear the echo of another life ending. They led the horses through the trees and each felt a chill up their spine at the sound of gunfire. They'd been hearing it all day.

"That's them," Sam said. "I saw them meet up with a group at the mouth of the canyon. I assumed it was too dark to bring them down."

"Only an Indian could guide them through," Theresa said, her voice filled with disdain that her own people would help the American murderers.

"They must have some kind of plan to be picked up and transported from there," Sam guessed, "unless we can get them before sunrise."

246

Theresa agreed. "Maybe four hours before dawn. After that, they're gone."

Leo stood in the middle of the trees and watched the exchange between Sam and Theresa. He couldn't believe his ears. After all they'd been through—explosions, getting shot at, losing a tooth, hell, even the kid almost bit the dust from a knife wound not two miles down the road—and still they wanted more. To do more.

"What?" he started. "What are you guys talking about? The guy that killed your grandfather is already dead, okay? I'm not going to get my money back, we have no shot at the reward money, Wills is back with his family. Our job is done here."

Sam stared at his brother. To a cop it was so simple. "Do you see anybody else out here who is going to go after them, Leo?"

"What's that got to do with anything, Sam?" Leo asked, his voice rising.

"I'm a cop," Sam said, angry that he had to spell it out to him. "I don't get to walk away."

"Sam, you're not a cop. You got suspended."

"I'm not asking you to go. Stay with the kid."

Upon hearing himself referenced, Douglas acted alert, although really it was the tree that was holding him up. "I told you I'm fine," he said weakly.

The sight of the injured kid, covered in his own blood and almost slurring from exhaustion, sent Leo into a tailspin. How could Sam be so reckless, so selfish? Leo felt a confusing mix of emotions: anger, sadness, hysteria, stress. Some of these feelings felt old, dating back to childhood. Others were very new.

"Oh, that's just great. You're going to get the kid killed, too. Just when I was starting to like your dumb ass. No," Leo yelled, turning to Sam. "I'm not letting you take him with you. Look at his leg—it's about to fall off. What are you going to do, carry him?"

Sam had had enough. "Jesus, Leo. Shut up."

Leo couldn't shut up. He was too far gone. All of them were. This entire adventure was just one big shit storm, and Sam didn't seem to want to let it end. No matter that guns were still going off somewhere in the dark, that people were still being killed.

"No. I won't shut up. It's crazy, Sam."

Silence fell over the group, seemingly over the entire desert. It was as if the gunshot they heard had unleashed a torrent within Leo; a dam somewhere inside of him burst. He'd been here before. He'd been here with Sam before, with people they loved in danger and Sam doing what he always did best: whatever the hell he wanted.

Leo got up in Sam's face, a quiet intensity vibrating between them.

"You know what, Sam? It baffles me that you aren't capable of walking away from being a cop yet you're completely fine with walking out on me and your little sister."

Sam looked curiously at Leo. There was a long beat as the years started to pile over Sam like a losing team on the goal line. They were not there and then they were, brought forth that easily by Leo's tirade. For Sam there was no present and no past—it all just *was,* here in the desert tonight. Leo was living it, and now so was he. For the first time, Sam saw to the core of it after all these years.

"So, that's what this is all about, Leo?"

"You left us alone with him," Leo said, every word a dagger meant to strike Sam in the heart. "You have absolutely no idea how bad he got after you left." Leo's voice was barely a whisper. Sam couldn't look him in the eye: all the anger, all the years were between them now. "Now,

Nina, you know her, she probably forgave you by now, but me?" Leo paused to catch his breath. "You were the one taking care of us, not him. I expected nothing from him, but you? You know the funny thing? Eventually he sobered up. *You* never came back, Sam."

Leo felt a catch in his throat as he walked away from Sam, who stood there frozen in the woods. He didn't respond. Sam didn't say anything at all.

"It's crazy how much you resent the guy because," Leo said, raising his voice to a full-throated scream, "you're just like him, Sam!"

Before the words had even left Leo's mouth, Sam was on him, charging at him like a bull. He grabbed Leo by the collar and slammed him against the nearest tree. He didn't notice Leo had the wind knocked out of him, or that his feet were no longer touching the dirt. At that moment, he didn't care. Sam was surrounded by his anger, absolutely overcome with it. His arms were not his own, his legs not his own; the fist ready to bash Leo's face into an unrecognizable pulp, that didn't belong to him, either.

The trees seemed to bend away from Sam, fearful of the utter rage coming off him in waves.

Theresa held Douglas back, almost for that very same reason—fear of what would happen to the young kid in his weakened state.

The only one not flinching or taking a protective stance was Leo. Pinned against the tree, barely able to draw a breath, Leo stared at his brother, his gaze unblinking. This was the monster he knew, the one he grew up with. The one he recognized.

"Come on, I got you last. What are you gonna do, Sammy? Do it! Do it!" Leo pushed back at Sam. "C'mon! *Hit me. Hit me!*"

And there it was. Those two little words stopped Sam dead in his tracks. Those two words took Sam back to Captain Haymer's office, to the thought he had of Leo just before he got suspended. It took him back to the room, the television monitor, the frozen face of a madman hell-bent on doing the "right" thing regardless of the consequences or who got hurt or who got in the way. Those two words were the thruway from their childhood to the present day, the one action that linked this entire mess together.

But Sam realized he didn't want that anymore. And he realized for the first time that Leo was right.

He backed down, releasing his grip on Leo, letting his fists unclench as he drew in a deep breath. His arms belonged to him once again, his fists the same.

He looked at his brother's face in a new light. It was not a loud, obnoxious failure of a bail bondsman that he saw standing in the desert at night. It was a scared and hurt little kid. A kid who got left behind.

"I was seventeen years old," Sam explained, his voice now quiet and even. "If I'd a stayed, I would've killed him. I'm sorry." That was all the explanation Sam had to offer. That was all he was going to give.

With that, Sam headed off into the darkness. The others soon followed, gathering the horses. Theresa did not speak—she didn't know the words in their language for this. Douglas hobbled after her, gently leading his horse. Leo slumped down in a ball near the tree and watched them go.

No one said good-bye. No one said much of anything. No one noticed that, once again, Leo was getting left behind.

Chapter
THIRTY-ONE

Sam, Douglas, and Theresa, just a trio now, made their way through the woods and into the beginnings of the canyons. They rode through the night, taking breaks only to rest the horses. Douglas's injured leg had stopped bleeding, but the pain persisted, and so he followed along in silence, wanting to play the role of the good brother now that Leo was gone. No one spoke about what happened earlier, Sam's fight with Leo and the ugly things that were said. Douglas had thought Sam was going to take Leo's head off—literally remove his head from his body—but somehow Sam managed to rein it in. Neither he nor Theresa had ever seen anyone like that—so quick to fly into a rage, so much strength and power lingering just under the surface—and so they stayed silent on the matter. They had enough to contend with in finding the kidnappers, in making their way through the canyons.

They had come across the body just before dawn—a stout man with glasses lying shot and dead in the bushes. Sam had searched the wallet and found a name—Nicolas Canton—to go along with it. A backpack with a shattered laptop lay nearby, and it wasn't difficult to figure out that Canton was on the wrong end of a double cross. But it caused them to increase their speed, the need to find these criminals all the greater since finding another of their victims, and Douglas's leg throbbed incessantly now.

Dawn broke high and bright over the canyons, revealing the tall and imposing jagged cliffs, surrounded in dust and dirt. It was the most barren landscape they had seen yet, all humpback mountains and steep, unsteady trails, with small pockets of dead or dying brush.

Theresa surveyed the landscape she knew so well. Her father and his father before him had taught her this land, its many paths and crevices, when she was a young girl. Her first feelings of pride came from learning these canyons, from naming each and every jagged finger of mountain. It disturbed her that something once considered so solemn and sacred, beautiful in its own austere and unique way, was being corrupted by these encroaching Americans and their greedy, murderous ways. And worse, they were using Indian guides to take them through it.

She stood on the plateau and turned back to Douglas and Sam, still on horseback. "It will be difficult for the horses the rest of the way in the canyons." They would have to go forward on foot. They would lose more time.

Just then a sound echoed through the canyons. In the midst of its ancient rock formations, desert brush, and bright, unending sky came a shiny metal object, glittering in the distance.

Sam trained his eyes on the flying object. The blunt whir of the helicopter's engine and its blades were soon pronounced enough. The helicopter bore no official markings, no law-enforcement signs whatsoever. Which meant to Sam it must be private issue. And probably not belonging to the good guys.

"You think they're looking for him?" Douglas asked.

"I don't know. It's not military."

Suddenly a flare shot up from the base of one of the canyons, a lighted wire pointing its way up into the sky. Sam guessed it to be a marker rather than an SOS. It had to be Nealon, enacting the Mexican desert's version of hailing a cab.

"Maybe that's his way out," Sam said. He turned to Douglas and Theresa. "Head down to the canyons in case he doubles back."

Theresa looked confused. "They won't be able to land in the bottom of the canyons."

Sam was a step ahead of her. "They're going to pull him out." Sam turned the horse around and took off along the top of the ridge toward the area where the flare was fired, leaving Theresa and Douglas to lead their horses as far as they could down into the canyons. He only hoped they could reach Nealon in time. The helicopter was moving quickly over the skyline and with the flare in sight would probably reach Nealon in less than five minutes, even with the difficult terrain.

Sam rode the horse hard, staying high on the ridge for as long as he could. The helicopter stayed in his sight line, burning in the heat of the morning and fighting the up swells of occasional desert winds. Sam could see where it was heading: just over the bluff he could see the lingering white smoke of the flare, extending down to a drop-off of at least fifty feet.

He jumped off the horse and started running up the bluff, his boots dancing through rocks and stone and prickly shrub. Theresa was right: there was no way the horses could follow.

The helicopter began to hover over the opening of a deep, shaded canyon. It lowered a weighted cable down to Nealon, who stood waiting for the cable ride that was now his ticket to freedom. The flash drive was in his pocket: 500 million dollars that he no longer had to share with anyone. Rodriguez, Bermutti, probably Bertram and the others: they were all dead. He was the last man standing. Winner takes all.

The cable gathered at the bottom of the canyon like a coiled snake. Nealon placed his foot in the sling and held on to the black cable, signaling for the pilot to pull him up. Within seconds, Nealon's feet were off the ground. The two Indian guides nearby, both armed with rifles at the ready, watched the crazy American begin to be lifted up into the sky.

At that moment, Sam reached the top of the

bluff and could see, straight ahead, the mouth of the cliff. The helicopter hovered there in midair, a cable stretching below it, within possible striking distance from the side of the cliff.

Sam saw his one chance to stop Nealon, to put an end to all of this bloodshed and murder, and he decided to take it.

Sam launched into a dead run. He threw down the large cowboy hat as he ran, leaving it to the desert brush. He whisked off the trench coat, riddled with dust and his own dried blood, and it pooled behind him in a heap. His boots pounded the dry ground of the canyon, letting off explosions of dust in his wake. He had no other costumes, no other thoughts, nothing left to leave behind. And it felt good.

He reached the end of the cliff and, using all of his considerable strength, leaped off the edge of the canyon, reaching for thin air.

His body moved over the space between the end of the cliff and the helicopter with nothing below him. Sam was airborne, traveling far out into the space through only momentum and steel will. He reached one of the landing struts of the helicopter and grabbed on for dear life, his lower body swinging forward past his chest, his feet almost reaching the opposite strut from the strength of his jump. His legs swung below the rest of his body as Sam, wrapping his thick arms around the metal strut, dangled in midair.

Sam's weight threw off the balance of the helicopter. The pilot labored to keep the machine steady, swaying from side to side as Sam held on. Far below him, Nealon, with only the foot sling to offer balance, tried to do the same.

The Indian guides watched Sam cross the divide between the cliff and the helicopter and land on the strut. He was a sitting duck, hanging in the air with no backup, no protection. They each raised their rifles and started taking shots at him. The bottom of the helicopter was soon riddled with bullet holes, adding to its instability. Sam knew he was lucky to avoid those shots but he also knew his luck wouldn't hold out forever. Sooner or later their aim would be true. And he'd get a mouthful of lead.

Perched behind a large boulder up above the canyon, Theresa climbed as silently as she could, closer to the edge of the clearing. She got a strong foothold against the rocks and raised her rifle, aiming squarely at the first guide. It almost felt unnatural for her to fire at one of her own people, but she figured they'd given up the right to loyalty when they joined forces with the men who killed her grandfather. She set the guide in her sights and fired. The bullet was a direct hit, knocking him squarely in the chest. He went down in a cloud of red dust.

The second guide followed the shot's trajectory and saw the woman with the gun. He aimed and fired at her. She let out a moan, falling backward and dropping her gun.

Douglas appeared above them all, across the mouth of the canyon. He saw Theresa go down and fired two shots at the second guide, who took both bullets and fell down from his perch on the rocks, his body hitting the hard dust.

"Are you okay?" he yelled to Theresa, concern filling his voice.

"I'm fine," she yelled back, holding her arm. "Just go!" She motioned for him to help Sam, who was still hanging off the side of the hovering helicopter. But Douglas's position was too high, and his leg too injured, and he struggled to hobble over to help his brother.

The helicopter pilot fought to maintain control over his craft as it continued to sway from side to side, injured both by the bullets and

Sam's added weight. Sam summoned up all his strength and moved across the strut, reaching for the cable leading down from the cabin. He grabbed onto it and let go of the strut, swinging onto the cable like it was a vine. He wrapped his boots around the cable, directly above Nealon. Like a fireman on a pole, Sam careened down the cable at an accelerating speed, heading straight for Nealon. With nowhere to go, lingering in the air by only the foot sling, Nealon could not do anything except brace himself for the impact.

Sam's body crashed into Nealon with the force of an angry linebacker. The violent collision ripped them both from the cable and sent them crashing hard to the dusty floor of the canyon.

The helicopter, now free of their weight, bid a hasty retreat out of the canyon, disappearing against the large, blaring desert sun.

Both men hit the ground and immediately lost their bearings. Nealon's sunglasses went flying and cracked against the rocks. He landed on his back in a cloud of dust, his eyes shut against the pain of the fall. Sam landed on his side, taking the ground like a hard jab to the ribs. The wind was knocked out of him and his vision was blurry from the crash and the dust. He felt like he had just slammed into a side of beef or had been on the wrong side of a heavyweight fight.

Sam rose first, trying to catch his breath, bent at the waist and coughing up half the canyon floor from his lungs. Nealon, perhaps ten feet away now, slithered up like a snake, his long arm reaching behind his waistband and pulling out a Sig Sauer. He had the drop on Sam, whose vision returned in time to see Nealon's gun trained directly on him. At close range.

There was a long pause as both men stood and stared at each other. The Iceman versus the cop. A thin smile grew over Nealon's craggy face.

"Good morning," Nealon said dryly. "What brings you to this neck of the woods?"

Sam still struggled to catch his breath. "You're under arrest," he said. The insanity of the comment only caught up with him after the fact. There he was, bruised and bloodied and unarmed, staring down the sight of a gun trained on him.

Nealon let out a laugh filled with malice and irony. He said nothing, only raised the gun right to Sam's chest. The Iceman liked to kill in cold blood, and this one, for him, would be no different.

Sam held his ground, determined to face his end with dignity. He wondered if it would be Theresa or Douglas to find him first, what a tough thing that would be for the kid. He wondered what they would tell Nina, and how she would keep them all together without him around. All of these thoughts flew into his head at the speed of light, in an instant, as Nealon's finger began to squeeze the trigger.

The sound of a gun echoed throughout the canyon. It was loud and violent, and it shook small rocks from the loose gravel walls surrounding them.

Nealon's body buckled under the weight of it, collapsing in a heap on the floor of the canyon.

Sam was stunned, and he was still intact. He looked up to the top of the ravine, where his brother Leo stood holding a rifle. A smoking rifle.

Sam looked at Leo, then back at the dead man lying before him. Leo had just saved his life.

"Never walk out on family, Sam," he yelled from the high shelf of dirt.

"You're absolutely right," Sam agreed.

Leo raised his rifle in the air, the metal piece framed by the vibrant blue sky. "Woo-hoo!" he yelled at the top of his lungs.

Douglas, limping and still in pain, finally made his way to Sam. He looked up at Leo. "Nice going!" Then, trying to remember, he said, "What was it, Horse?"

"No," Leo said, shaking his head but still smiling. "It's Hoss. And I'm not Hoss."

Sam joined in. "I can't be Hoss. I'm the oldest. By process of elimination, you're Hoss."

Leo studied Sam for a long beat, then figured this was a fight he couldn't win. He'd let Sam have this one. "Fine—if only by process of elimination. I can live with that." And he meant it.

Chapter
THIRTY-TWO

Theresa's house appeared like even more of an oasis, given what they all had been through. They were grateful for the chance to clean up, to wash the dust of the desert and the canyons off their hands and faces. Even Leo managed to clean up a bit, although there was nothing here he could do about his missing tooth. They cleaned and bandaged the kid's leg. Sam checked out Theresa's bullet wound—nothing too serious, more of a graze, and wrapped her arm gently in a sling. Considering the body count left behind, they all could have gotten off a lot worse.

Less bloody but still bruised, the three brothers made their way back to the Jeep to say their good-byes. They followed the stone walk past the manicured lawn to the graveled area where Sam had parked the Jeep. Hard to believe it was just days ago they came here to interrogate Theresa. Now she felt like one of them. She felt like family.

"Are you sure there's nothing more we can do for you?" Sam asked.

Leo jumped in. "Yeah, the FBI says we're good for two hundred and fifty K of the reward money. And in my opinion, I think you more than earned your share. That's twenty-five percent."

He remembered suddenly about Sam and Douglas and didn't want to once again put his foot in his mouth where Theresa was concerned.

"I mean, I'm assuming it's okay with you guys."

"Seems fair," Sam agreed.

"Absolutely," Douglas said.

She dismissed them all with a slight wave. "No. Please, I'm fine."

Leo hugged her gently. But he was still awkward around her, and he leaned on her bad shoulder just as she touched his broken rib. They both winced at the same time.

"I'm sorry," he said, "I know—it's been a couple of days . . ."

But this time she smiled, amused by his awkwardness.

She walked over to Sam and gave him a hug and a kiss for luck.

That only left Douglas.

"I'll miss you," he said earnestly. Their hug lasted longer than the others'. "I'd like to come back and visit. Leo is going to lend me his Spanish tapes."

Theresa smiled at him. Her eyes were clear and bright, her smile warm and open. Douglas had never seen anything so beautiful. "I think I would like that very much."

He took her hand as she kissed his cheek. "Take care," he said. But he meant so much more.

Douglas climbed into the Jeep. It was ruined by mud and dust. They drove away, Douglas keeping his eyes on Theresa for as long as he could. It hurt him to see her standing there, alone now, remembering all that she had sacrificed to help them. But he also knew that one day, one day very soon, he would be back.

Chapter
THIRTY-THREE

Nina never thought it would be like this. She never thought she'd feel this way. She worked so hard to bring them together. Watching her father get sick, watching him prepare to leave them all, she had to come up with something. Something to bring them back.

And they were back. She was so glad to have them back, to at least see they were safe, she forgot all about the other thing, the other business that had been plaguing her thoughts since her three brothers left for Mexico City. She had spent most of the week wondering what to do, and now they were here. Back. Safe.

Yet different. A family.

Nina watched them sitting at the table, once

again congregated at the local bar but this time only sipping coffee, still exhausted from the trip. She watched them all speaking to one another, smiling, laughing, talking and not shouting, and in the thirty minutes since they sat down not one fight had broken out. She stared at the three brothers she used to think of as boys. But here, today, they were something else entirely.

There was Leo, a bit bruised and beat up, but with a light behind his eyes. She'd promised to find him a dentist for the missing tooth, but he just nodded and said, "Thanks," and went back to the story he was telling, something about standing up to a bunch of thugs in the desert. He threw his head back and laughed, and she felt fifteen again. She hadn't seen him laugh like that in a long time.

And there was Douglas, the new kid, the one she barely knew, behaving like he'd been here all along. He walked with a slight limp, his leg sewn up and heavily bandaged. His long, blond hair was tucked behind his ears, and the rim of his left eye was bruised and blue, but his youth was unmistakable, his energy and good nature infectious. He was already finishing Leo's sentences and for some reason calling him "Horse."

And then Sam—solid, stoic Sam. Nina wondered about him most of all. He kept his large hands folded in front of him on the table, but something about him was different, too. That would take longer for her to figure out.

The image of all of them together at the table moved her deeply. She started to tear up, not for what she saw but for what she had to do next. She flicked an errant tear away and fingered the silver cross around her neck. She hated this. The business of lying.

"There is no money," she suddenly blurted much too loudly, afraid that the words wouldn't leave her throat. There was a very long pause. "There never was. It was the only way to bring you all together."

There. She said it. She hoped they would understand, that they would see how desperate she was to have her brothers back again, and how that desperation made her come up with the stupid plan. The money, the lawyer, the business. All of it was fake. But this—what she was watching at this table today—that was not. That was real.

Leo, Douglas, and Sam sat stunned in their chairs. Still not one word in response, so she continued.

"Daddy really was a changed man. His final wish," Nina said, choking up, "was to bring you all together. That much was true."

Still nothing from her brothers. Nina began to sweat, waiting for the inevitable explosion that was sure to follow. She'd lose them. She was sure of it. She had brought them together, and now, because of her, they were going to be torn apart. Even worse than before.

"There was no other way," she said, her voice small and fragile. "I'm sorry."

Finally, of course, it was Leo who recovered his ability to speak first.

"You lied?" he yelled, the entire bar turning to look at their table. "You've never told a lie in your entire life! Me, I lie all the time, and Sam, he's a huge liar, and Douglas, the kid's a thief for Chrissakes, but you?" His voice cracked from the hysteria. "I believed you, Nina."

"I'm sorry, I'm so sorry," she said, the tears bursting forth. "I will go to Confession."

"Oh yeah. Confession," Leo mocked her. "Bless me, Father, for I have sinned, and it's all fine now. Are you kidding me? What are you going to do about us?"

"Leo," she said, regaining herself. "I'm sorry

you're angry. But the real question is: does the end justify the means? I mean, look at you all."

And with that, she looked right at Sam, who was still in a state of shock. He stared back at her and she saw it again: something had changed within him. At first she had taken his silence for anger but now she could see there was something else at work. His mind was racing. She could see the change moving all over his face. He nodded slightly and he, too, looked around the table.

"What about a private investigation agency?" Sam asked.

They all just stared at him, a collective *what?* coming off them.

"I don't follow," Nina said.

Leo and Douglas turned their attention to Sam. They had no idea what he was talking about, either.

"I'm a cop, Leo's a bail bondsman. We know criminals. The kid *is* a criminal."

"No!" Nina said firmly. "Absolutely not! I am not bringing you together so you can get killed."

But Leo was already getting the drift. "Wait a second. Are you actually suggesting that we still go into business together anyway?"

"Yeah," Sam said. "If you're going to do something, you want to succeed, you might as well be good at it, right?"

Douglas was already convinced. "I like it. I'm in."

"That is not what Daddy wanted," Nina said.

"The old man wanted us together. I hope that sorry son of a bitch is rolling over in his grave right now."

Nina groaned out loud and placed her head on the table, but only to hide the smile growing on her face. Nina never thought it would be like this. But now that it was—well, she didn't mind at all.

Chapter
THIRTY-FOUR

Los Angeles, California: City of Angels, city of everything. Ten million people living fast and breathing smog. But what these millions of people sometimes forget is that they have the best weather in the country, sometimes the world. They have the most diverse landscape of any major urban center: coastline, mountains, deserts, farmland. And while oftentimes, stuck in traffic or desperately clinging to a doorway during an earthquake, they feel like they have no connections, no ties, most of the time this isn't true. In a bustling city spread out from coastland to farmland to desert townships, there are often more elements that tie them together than they'll ever realize. A stranger at the bus stop could be a wanted fugitive—or, perhaps, a family member, a long-lost sibling, a brother never met. What was true about Los Angeles, the Carey siblings learned the hard way, was that in such a crowded and bustling city, the possibilities for connections were endless. You only had to look for them.

Nina had thought about that a lot over the past few weeks: endless possibilities. For the first time in a long while she felt the wonder and excitement of having a family: her three brothers, all nearby, all in touch, all getting along, and finally, all together.

She told her father about it just the other day, while placing flowers on his grave. She had wanted him to know that she'd accomplished what he asked her to do. She had brought his three sons together and by a miracle (well, by a great big lie, a murder, and a kidnapping scheme, to be more accurate) they had remained that way. She told her father about the family business they were going to start. Not her first choice, but still. Sam had an instinct about it, he told her later, and so she was going to follow that. She owed him that much.

Nina hurried down the block, keeping an eye on her surroundings. It was a forgotten block in an area she didn't know well, just southeast of downtown, not an area she would normally choose, but Leo had insisted. She rounded the corner to the alley, and that's where she saw it, hanging over the brick front doorway, in simple black-and-white letters: *Carey Brothers Private Investigators.*

She joined her brothers, who were standing in the alley watching the handyman hang the sign.

"How much reward money we got left after our expenses?" Leo asked.

Sam replied, "We covered your bond with two hundred fifty K. Plus the old man's ten K, minus expenses. Maybe twenty-five K left." Nina made a note to make sure she handled all of the accounting for their new family business.

"I still got six months left on the lease—paid in full," Leo boasted. The alley held on to that ripe smell, but he hoped the increased foot traffic would keep the bums away, at least during the daylight hours.

"It's a good central location," Douglas said, looking over his shoulder.

Nina had to laugh. "It's a dump."

Sam nudged his little sister. "Hey, this is your fault, Nina."

Nina looked up at the sign again. "Why is my

name not on it? Why just the brothers? I don't think that's very fair."

While Nina pleaded her case to Sam, Leo started humming. He started shuffling his feet, his voice getting louder and louder. The neighborhood knew Leo. They were used to this.

Sam, Douglas, and Nina all stared at Leo, now humming embarrassingly loud.

"What's that song?" Douglas asked.

Sam replied, "It's the theme song to *Bonanza*. Shut up, Leo. Nobody thinks it's funny."

Leo stopped humming long enough to answer back. "You shut up. It's hysterical."

Then he started humming again.

Sam tried to stop him, but Leo just hummed louder. So Sam did an about-face and started walking away from the alley. It only made Leo hum louder. As Douglas ran after his brother, Nina joined in, dancing around the alley with her brother, their voices echoing down the alley and out into the neighborhood, *their* neighborhood, the one that held their brand-new family business.